Th

The Garden Gate

Patsy Collins

To my gardening uncles –

Basil, Grahame and Linden Collins,
and Tony Ellison

Contents

1 Random Acts Of Kindness

Izzy glared at her lunch. Boringly healthy stuff again. Why was she bothering? Two weeks she'd stuck to this diet and gone for a brisk walk most evenings and so far she'd lost only three pounds. Nobody had even noticed. The snack trolley would be round in a minute; she might as well buy chocolate to cheer herself up.

She heard the tinkle of the bell which alerted the hungry to the presence of chocolate, crisps and other goodies in the corridor and left her desk. Halfway across the office a colleague blocked her way.

"You're looking good, Izzy. Have you lost weight?"

"I've been trying to."

"I think it shows in your face and you look healthier."

"Really? Thanks. I thought I might go for a quick walk before lunch."

Izzy only did a lap of the office building, but if she did that every day when the snack trolley came round it might help shift another pound.

After work she went shopping. The only item she purchased which wasn't included on her diet was a packet of biscuits for her brother who'd be visiting. Unfortunately his favourites were on a 'buy one get one free' promotion. Having spare biscuits in the house was a temptation she could do without.

Before Izzy in the checkout queue was an elderly lady. She didn't look well off and the few items she bought were all own label or reduced price. There was an exception; three tins of the best quality cat food.

After paying for her own food Izzy soon caught the lady up. She offered her the spare biscuits, explaining they were free and she was on a diet.

Yvonne was delighted with the cream-filled, chocolate covered biscuits. She had enough money to live on if she was careful, but the odd little luxury made all the difference. Now she really would invite her neighbour in for tea. She'd often thought about it and several times she'd almost done so, but lost her nerve at the last moment. Her neighbour might be busy, or perhaps feel she was being pushy, and besides, Yvonne had little to offer other than conversation and company.

Rita looked startled when she'd answered the door in response to Yvonne's knock.

"Hello, er, Yvonne isn't it? Is something wrong?"

"Not at all, I was about to have some tea and just wondered if you'd like to join me?"

"Tea?"

"Yes. Just a cup and a biscuit, if you have time?"

"I suppose I do."

Conversation was slow at first but by the time they'd finished the first cup and poured a second they were chatting like old friends.

"This has been lovely," Rita said once the tea and biscuits

were all gone. "Perhaps you'd come round to mine tomorrow afternoon? I love to bake and there seems so little point just for me."

"I would like that, but I'm afraid I couldn't return the favour. I'm no cook."

"Don't worry about that. Now tell me, what kind of cakes do you like best?"

When Rita's son made one of his rare visits, she told him all about her new friend.

"We have tea together most days now. It's fun creating tempting treats for her."

"I don't imagine she needs much persuading. This Bakewell tart is absolutely delicious. You've always been an excellent cook, Mother."

"Thank you, dear. I don't think she'd need much persuading in any case. Other than her cat she seems quite alone and I rather suspect the only times she eats properly are when she comes here. I've starting adding savoury quiches and pies to our afternoon teas and I do think she's looking less frail."

"That's kind of you."

"Not entirely. Yvonne might be short of cash, but she's full of interesting stories and good humour. The arrangement is good for both of us."

Mark nodded to show his agreement.

"I'd like us to do other things together. Perhaps days out to gardens or museums. From what she's said I'm sure she'd enjoy that and I know I would."

"That sounds an excellent plan, Mother. I can look up

some local places on the internet and print out bus and train timetables for you if you like. I'll be passing by on Tuesday and I could drop them in then."

"Yes please, love," Rita said although mostly because it meant she'd have another opportunity to see her son.

"Anything else I can do to help?"

"I could do with some advice. You know I'm not always tactful."

"Well..."

"The thing is, I don't know how I can pay without causing offence? We're both lonely and we needn't be if we can just stop the fact that one of us has more money than the other from getting in the way."

"I'll have a think and I'll ask Louise if she has any ideas."

"Thank you. How is she? Well I hope?"

"Yes, but very busy with work."

"Yes, I understand."

That evening Mark told his wife, "Mum had baked my favourite cake, ready for my visit."

"That was nice of her."

"It was and actually she was nice too. She's made friends with the lady next door and it seems to have done her the world of good. Mostly Mum talked about her. The nearest she came to moaning about anything was to say they were both lonely, but even then it was to say she'd thought of a cure."

"Really? Tell me."

Louise listened and offered suggestions. "There are some small gardens quite near my office that don't charge an entrance fee. They could use their free bus passes to get there and I could give them lunch in the canteen."

Mark squeezed her hand. "Mum would love that."

"Well, I really shouldn't avoid her completely and if she's cheered up a bit perhaps I won't want to."

Mark took the timetables and leaflets to his mother on the Tuesday as he'd promised. Later he told Louise, "Seems the change wasn't just a one off. She was still quite cheerful and didn't complain when I said I could only stay a few minutes."

A week later both Mark and Louise visited Rita. Mark gave his mother an envelope containing a membership card for a local horticultural organisation.

"With this, both you and your friend can get into dozens of places for nothing."

"Oh that's wonderful! You are clever, Mark. I wouldn't have thought of that."

"It was Louise's idea actually."

"Then thank you, my dear. And how are you? Mark's told me how busy you are at work. I do hope you enjoy it?"

"I do, yes. Actually it's calmed down a little now. Maybe you'd like to come and see me there?" She explained her plan for Rita and Yvonne to visit the local gardens and come to lunch.

"That sounds lovely."

Louise couldn't stop smiling at work the following morning. Now her mother-in-law was less of a grouch everything seemed so much better. Louise used to do all she could to avoid the woman which had made her feel guilty.

Mark too had hated visiting. It hurt him to see her so unhappy and hurt him more when she took it out on him by complaining the whole time he was there and then being upset that he didn't visit more frequently. The weight of that was always at the back of his mind.

Yesterday his mother had been positively cheerful. Her only concern was how to implement her plans without distressing her neighbour. Louise chuckled at her solution to that.

"Tell her your daughter-in-law isn't always that nice and you need her for moral support. Make her think she's doing you a favour."

Mark's mother had actually laughed. "Shall I say you complain about my cooking?"

Louise couldn't reply as she had a mouthful of the most gorgeous homemade chocolate cake, but she'd nodded her agreement.

Weirdly she was looking forward to the visit. It would be fun pretending to be nasty and only hiding it for the sake of that Yvonne lady. How strange she'd only be letting her dislike show just as she was no longer feeling it.

A big improvement in the lives of several people had all started with the new friend offering a cup of tea and friendly words. Maybe something like that could work on her colleague Sue? She'd been grouchy ever since she was diagnosed with high blood pressure and told to lose weight. Poor woman, it must be a struggle especially as they had access to an excellent canteen as well as the office being located close to several fast food outlets. Maybe a few words of encouragement might help?

Louise waited until lunchtime so she could seemingly bump into Sue by accident.

"Hi, Sue. Gosh you're looking good. You've lost weight haven't you?"

"You think so? I have been trying but it's difficult. Actually I was just about to give in and go out for a burger but you've persuaded me not to."

Sue put the money she'd been about to spend on a burger into the charity box. Maybe the money would help put a smile on someone's face?

2 Good Boy

Jamie wanted to play with the other boys, but couldn't risk it. If he was naughty, they'd send him away. They might say he was so naughty nobody could look after him.

The sun shone into his eyes, making him squint. Jamie longed to leave his red plastic seat on the patio. His bottom was numb. He wanted to stamp his feet until the pins and needles eased. Usually he loved being out in the garden; he could move about or stay still without being in anyone's way. Today though he wasn't just sharing the patch of ground and collection of bushes with Daniel and Lee.

He tilted his head so most of it was in the shade. It made his neck ache, but he didn't move again. People don't like it if you keep fidgeting. If he was noisy, they might become angry. If he got in the way or broke anything he might be punished. If he fell and hurt himself he might go to hospital and not be allowed back.

No one was talking to him; perhaps it would be all right to go now? Then he could run behind the barbecue, dodge past David, grab the ball and shoot through the rusty hoop on the garage wall. He'd never experienced the thrill of scoring the winning shot. He'd never been part of a team. It was safest just to stay quietly alone.

He wanted to ask if he might have another of the juicy, chunky sausages. The smell was still in the air, though they'd been cooling on the plate for the last thirty minutes. It was best just to sit still; they might not notice him so much.

"OK, Jamie?"

"Yes, thank you, Aunt Sheila."

"Had enough to eat?"

"Yes, thank you."

"Don't you want to go and play?"

"Would you like me to?"

"It's up to you, love."

Should he stay, or go and play? She was smiling. She didn't seem angry. He decided he must do something; she was waiting for him to move. He walked slowly to where David and Lee were taking turns trying to get the ball through the net. He watched and listened.

"Jamie is very quiet isn't he? Doesn't look like he gives you much trouble."

"Oh no, Jamie's a very good boy."

He knew he'd made the right decision this time. Aunt Sheila had said he was a good boy. That meant another meal tonight and a warm bed. He knew to be good was to be safe. The lady told him that.

"You're to stay with Sheila and Trevor Patterson. They have two boys, one a year older than you and one a year younger. I'm sure you'll like it there and if you're a good boy you may be able to stay."

He thought he'd been good at the last house. Sally and Simon Cattrell, his emergency foster parents, said he was, but they sent him away. His mother often had to hit him because he was so naughty. She said it was to teach him a lesson. He must have learnt, as the Cattrells never once hit him, not even a slap. They only made him go without food once. That was because he'd been sick. He knew he must never be sick but he couldn't help it. Maybe that was why they sent him away?

He knew he was naughty. His mother had told him often enough. That was why she left him alone sometimes. He was far too naughty to go with her. He didn't really mind being alone, at least he never got into any trouble. It was worse when he was left with his mother's friends. They frightened him and made him do things he didn't like. He couldn't tell anyone what happened. They said no one would believe him and he'd be punished for lying. So he tried to forget. He only remembered occasionally, when it was late and he couldn't sleep. His thin body would shake then, with the effort of holding in his sobs. You shouldn't cry when you were safe in your bed. If you did you might wake someone up. If you were crying for no reason, then they'd provide one. You could cry then. You could cry until you slept.

He'd heard people say she was a bad mother but he knew this wasn't true. She'd had to punish him when he misbehaved. His mother was special. She deserved better than to be poor and stuck with a whinging child to look after. She could have been something if she hadn't had him. He'd ruined her looks and figure. He thought she was beautiful and had told her. She'd been pleased with him then. She kissed him and said he wasn't such a bad kid really. They had gone to McDonald's together; he'd been allowed a burger and some very thin chips and a great big milkshake. It was pink and so thick he could hardly suck it through the straw. She asked him if she was a good mother and promised to look after him better. On the way home, she met a friend.

"Heather, I've got some good stuff. Real pure."

"I don't have any money and I've my son to think about."

"I've got a couple of pals who'll find a way for you to pay." He gave Jamie a £5 note. "Get yourself some fish and chips for tea. Your mum'll be a bit late home."

He'd not seen his mother for two days. Jamie spent the money on lots of crisps, a fruit pie and a pint of milk so he was fine.

He tried so hard to be good, but it was difficult. Often he simply didn't know what he should do. They only taught you reading and writing at school. There was no one to say how he should behave. You were just supposed to know. If he was in her way, he was wrong. If he kept away from her, she'd become angry. If he didn't eat all the food he was given she threw the plate at him. If he was greedy and asked for food, when he'd been given none, he'd be punished. If he missed school, he knew there'd be trouble from the teachers and his mother. Sometimes he couldn't go; he knew no one must ever see his bruises or the burns caused by her cigarettes. Other people didn't always understand why he had to be punished.

The last time she went away, he didn't see her for a week. When the electric ran out it was dark and cold. He got so hungry he stole food from a shop. He was caught and the police came. They shut him in a room with a lady. Knowing he'd be punished, he cried. The lady didn't hit him; she gave him a sandwich and a bottle of Coke. He was so surprised that he answered her questions. He knew you must never tell

11

the police anything but he didn't think she was the police. She didn't have a uniform. She said she was a social worker. She showed him a card with her picture on it. His mother said social workers were do-gooding busybodies. He couldn't remember if you were allowed to talk to them or not, but perhaps she would do good to him.

He ate the sandwich so quickly he didn't notice what filling it contained. He gulped down half the Coke in one go but sipped the remainder slowly. He let each bubble pop on his tongue, exploding its sweetness into him. He kept it in his mouth until it was so warm and flat he could no longer feel it. He forgot his problems and just enjoyed the feeling of no longer being hungry, no longer being cold and alone. The lady already knew a lot about him. He asked if she knew his mum and if she was coming back soon.

"Yes I've met your mother. I'm sorry, you can't see her for a while," the lady said. "She's not very well. She wants you to be looked after properly. I told her I'd make arrangements."

He'd been so naughty his mother could no longer look after him. It must have been because he'd shown the police where they lived. He knew they should never be let inside the flat, but they said they were looking for his mum. He'd believed them. He hadn't realised it was a trick to make her send him away.

The police didn't take him away from the Cattrells, it was the lady, the one who was a social worker. She told him to go with the Pattersons and be good. He tried really hard, but it wasn't working. Aunt Sheila kept asking him things.

"Are you happy?" "What would you like to do today?" or,

"What is your favourite game?"

Jamie didn't know the answers. He knew he liked the garden though. It was like the playground at school; not shut in, but still safe. Sometimes he was there on his own. That was the best. Sometimes, like now, Daniel and Lee were there too.

The brothers stopped playing and asked if he'd like to join in. He didn't know what to say. It wasn't fair. He'd never been able to please his mother, or the Cattrells. Now he was at the Pattersons' house. There were four of them, how could he possibly hope to please them all? Jamie cried. He didn't even try to control himself. The sobs became louder until he howled, close to hysteria. The boys ran, calling their mother.

Aunt Sheila came. If he'd noticed her speeding towards him with arms outstretched, he'd have been frightened. She held him very tight, rocking him against her warm body. She called instructions to her husband but never let go of Jamie.

Soon, everyone else was gone. It was just Jamie in Sheila's arms sat on the ground against the overgrown laurel hedge. They stayed there a long time and then the lady came. He thought she'd come to take him away and clung to Sheila, begging her not to let the lady near him.

"So you want to stay?"

He looked at her to see if she was angry. She wasn't so he nodded his head.

The lady came often and they all talked a lot. David and Lee taught him to play ball. Uncle Trevor taught him to ride a bicycle and Aunt Sheila taught him to smile. Gradually he told them about his mother and how he was naughty, that's why nobody wanted him. Aunt Sheila and Uncle Trevor told him he was really a good boy; it wasn't his fault his mother couldn't cope. They told him his mother had been ill. She'd taken drugs but they hadn't made her better. Uncle Trevor said he didn't need to know about all that yet; he just needed to know he had a home with them now.

One cold rainy day Jamie didn't go to school. Instead, he and Auntie Sheila and Uncle Trevor got dressed in dark clothes. The lady came in her car and took them to a church. It was to say goodbye to his mother. She wasn't there. He saw some of the people who'd lived in the same flats. They said they were sorry, but it was all for the best.

Jamie was sad his mother wasn't there. He hoped she was happy now she didn't have to look after him. When they went outside to look at some flowers he said goodbye to her anyway. That made Aunt Sheila cry, so he gave her a hug and then she was happy again.

Jamie was adopted by the Pattersons. He went to school with his new brothers. When they came home, his new mother was waiting for them.

Sometimes David or Jamie or Lee would be naughty and they would be told off. Sometimes, they would be punished. Perhaps they weren't allowed sweets for a few days, or were sent early to bed. Aunt Sheila always explained what they'd done wrong and how to behave better next time. They were never hit or burnt or abandoned. They were never hungry or cold or frightened.

Most of the time Jamie was a very good boy.

3   Family Tree

Julie threw the gardening magazine across the room. "Families! Can't chose them, can't get away from them."

"Oh dear, what's wrong?" her husband, Andrew, asked. He bent to retrieve the magazine from where it had landed and placed it with the, abandoned and still unfinished, homework of their two sons.

"Julie Fisher née Cordingley," she muttered through clenched teeth. "It's not enough that I've studied for years, am highly qualified, have researched and written that article, oh no! What's important is that I'm the cousin of the great and good Giles Cordingley."

"I'll make a cup of tea," Andrew said.

Julie hoped there was enough sugar to last until she could get to the supermarket on Friday. She couldn't go food shopping before she got paid because an hour ago Joe had announced he needed new trainers by Wednesday.

"Why couldn't you have told me earlier?" she'd demanded.

"They didn't break until today," he'd informed her.

She couldn't really blame him for not mentioning they were getting worn as she hadn't noticed that herself. She could see it now though; he'd left the evidence on the living room floor. Julie dropped them in the bin, then returned to the sofa and read her article properly. When Andrew returned with tea and biscuits, she said, "You were right."

"I didn't say anything." He took the magazine from her and scanned through her piece on re-establishing elm trees into Britain.

"No, but you were thinking it. I've overreacted. My cousin is a better dendrologist than me so obviously every time I write anything about trees he has to get a mention." She sighed again. In a way she'd always been in the shadow of Giles. Her cousin was a little older, and as a girl she'd looked up to him. At school she was compared to him and encouraged to reach the high standards he set. She probably owed what success she'd achieved to a kind of one-sided rivalry with him. Her grades matched his until she reached university and met Andrew. Her priorities changed and although she followed Giles' footsteps with her job choice, she was always a little behind him. On a lower professional branch, so to speak.

Giles teased and reminded her of this frequently. He was always offering his help, as though to imply she needed it. He often cited her research in his reports or otherwise drew attention to his good, but not quite so good, cousin.

"That's it, I've had enough!" Julie jumped up and walked out the room.

"What are you doing now?" Andrew asked.

"I'm going to have it out with him and ask him to lay off."

She rang Giles and explained her grievance.

"I don't understand, Julie."

"No, I don't suppose you bother to read anything by someone as inferior as me."

"Julie, you're not inferior. I admire you greatly and read all your work."

"Oh don't patronise me." She hung up.

When she returned, Andrew looked up enquiringly.

"He thinks I'm making a fuss over nothing too. He acts as though he's genuinely proud of me and our relationship and says he's not trying to show off."

"Perhaps that's true?" Andrew tentatively suggested.

Julie glared at him.

"When he refers to your work he's always respectful and fully credits you."

"Yes, I suppose so."

"And I've read this article." He held up the magazine. "It doesn't mention Giles at all. Maybe using your maiden name was just to confirm that you're the same Julie whose work they've read and admired previously."

"Maybe." She was quiet for a moment. "Oh dear, Andrew, I haven't been fair to Giles have I?"

Tactfully, her husband didn't reply.

"Trouble is, I know he's better than me and I don't like it."

"You're much prettier though, love."

"Nice try. I was as good as him once. Motherhood seems to have melted my brain. Well, perhaps not motherhood exactly, but all the little things that go with it."

"Little things like childbirth, nappy changing and three a.m. feeds?"

"No, I was expecting that and an interruption to my career for maternity leave, but it never ends does it? I'm always nagging them to do their homework and constantly having to find new trousers because they're growing faster than the grass and there's their sports activities to keep up with and...

See, it all comes down to families."

Julie decided she should make her apology to Giles in person. It wasn't his fault she couldn't live up to his high standards. The rivalry had always been mostly on her side. Giles had helped her as much as he could, especially in the early days of her career when he'd nicknamed her Sapling. Since then she'd allowed her jealousy to push him away. She hadn't been to his home in years.

Giles was obviously surprised to see Julie, but greeted her warmly and invited her in. His house was a tip; he had to move a stack of journals before she could sit.

"Would you like coffee?"

Julie removed several sections of tree from the table so there was room to set down the mugs. She forced herself to ignore the interesting way fungus had worked its way under the bark so it could feed off the tree's sap.

They drank the coffee black because he'd forgotten to buy milk.

Julie made her apology, despite Giles' protests that it was all his fault.

"I never realised my attitude might upset you. I'm sorry about that. Trees never get upset even when I chop bits off and sometimes I forget people have feelings."

"Think of us as weeping willows."

"I'll try that. Are you hungry? I could do beans on toast, they're all I've got. Actually, I can't cook anything else."

"Maybe I should give you a cookery lesson?"

"I'd like that. I'm hopeless about everything except

dendrology."

"Yes, but you're the best there is at that."

"Because I do nothing else. I don't have a life other than trees. When I said I admire you, it's true. I'm so impressed with the way you cope with a home, husband, lovely children. I wish I had enough balance for a life instead of just an obsession."

"I know just what you need; a family! Come to lunch tomorrow. I promise there won't be a baked bean in sight and the kids will distract you from all thoughts of work, except maybe helping Andrew build them a tree house."

4 Letting Things Grow

"You doing anything on Saturday?" Tony asked. "Louise and I could do with you if not."

"Count me in for whatever it is," Ryan said.

"Great. We're having a sort of dinner party and there's this lovely girl we'd like you to meet. We're sure you're perfect for each other."

Ryan scowled at the phone. He'd thought they wanted help with decorating or the garden. "Sounds very posh," he said about the dinner party.

"Not this one. Everyone's bringing something to eat or drink and you don't need to dress up. Could you bring a couple of chairs and plates and all that?"

A dinner party involving mismatched furniture and crockery he could probably handle. In theory if the party included a nice girl who might possibly be interested in him that should make it better. He would like a nice girlfriend and eventually wife and children but time was running out, especially for a man who didn't like to rush into things. He was over thirty and had never had a serious relationship. Tony and Louise said that was because girls got fed up waiting.

"I understand you don't want to get hurt, but by avoiding the chance of rejection, you miss any chance of being accepted," Tony said.

Ryan saw the truth in that, but he also saw he wasn't much of a catch: tall and gangly with mud coloured hair and eyes. He only earned just over minimum wage despite having been a reliable employee for the same place since leaving school. The old people's home where he was gardener, handyman and driver simply couldn't afford more.

Money didn't guarantee happiness anyway. Despite the lack of money he'd had a fantastic childhood. His parents, particularly his dad, had really been fun. They showed him how to be happy with very little. They had each other though, Ryan had no one to love like his parents had loved each other, or Tony loved Louise.

Ryan was never lonely, but he longed for one special person to love. He thought he could be a good husband to the right woman, if such a person existed. He could be a good father too, he was sure. Ryan imagined a little boy he could teach to dig and grow and build and mend things.

Having been tricked into accepting the dinner party invitation, Ryan made the most of it and the opportunity it represented. Tony and Louise knew him well and had never tried to pair him with anyone before. Maybe the girl really would be right for him? He didn't buy new clothes but wore the smartest he had and took care with his shave and getting every scrap of dirt from under his fingernails. She'd see him at his best, but it would be the real Ryan.

As he wasn't much of a cook, he'd offered to bring a salad. He gathered bags of fresh early leaves, radish and onions from his allotment. To these he added sprigs of parsley, sorrel, thyme and a big bunch of chives. He also selected armfuls of flowers; flamboyant tulips, delicate snowflakes, sprays of richly scented sarcococca and wallflowers.

Ryan set off early, so Louise could use the herbs in her recipe and they'd have time to arrange the flowers. He'd not been there long when Petra arrived. She helped him with the flowers and to prepare the salad and easily persuaded him to part with a few chives to snip over the onion tartlets she'd made as a starter. They chatted easily together as they worked. Ryan didn't get nervous until the other guests arrived. It then became clear that Petra was the girl Tony and Louise wanted him to meet.

They were right that she was lovely. He wasn't judging just on looks either. She was very nice to talk to, happy to help her hosts prepare and, based on those tartlets, a great cook too. No way would she be interested in him.

As Ryan and Tony hastily washed the starter plates, so dessert could be served, Tony asked, "So, do you like Petra?"

"Very much."

"So you'll ask her out?"

"She won't be interested."

"Go on, ask. What's the worst that could happen?"

Ryan had got bad reactions before, but he supposed Petra would be polite in front of their hosts. He shrugged.

"Look, she's a bit like you… not much confidence. If you ask her out it'll help with that even if she says no."

"All right, I'll ask."

He waited until the other guests had gone and he and Petra had helped clear away. "Would you come out with me one evening?"

Petra hesitated but after Louise muttered something in her

ear, she said, "OK, but not for too long."

He took her to the pictures. He hoped she would enjoy the film if not his company and he wouldn't have to say much. It seemed to go OK. He thought she might want to rush off straight away, but she came for a drink when he tentatively suggested it.

He told her about his job and she seemed interested. "My garden is a real mess, I don't have a clue what to do with it."

"I could come and have a look if you like?"

"No!"

"Right."

"I mean it's nice of you to offer but I couldn't impose. It's been a lovely evening, thank you but I'd better go now." She kissed his cheek before she left. It felt nice, but seemed like a very final goodbye.

Tony rang him a few days later and asked, "What's the problem?"

"She's not interested in seeing me again."

"That's what she said about you. Both of you seem to think you're not good enough for each other, but we can see you're perfect."

"Why wouldn't she think she was good enough? If there's something wrong with her it can't be much as I never noticed."

"Not wrong, no. She was in a relationship before that went badly wrong. I promised not to say... Look we introduced you but we can't do everything for you. Call her for goodness' sake."

Ryan did. He asked her to come out for a meal.

"Can I think about it?"

To his surprise she rang back and agreed. That was encouraging. In a way it was better than an instant acceptance as that might just have been because she felt pressured into it. Clearly she didn't like that. Petra must have thought he was being too pushy by offering to do the garden. Understandable. Going out with someone is very different from letting them into your home.

After a few dates Ryan realised he was falling in love. Petra seemed to rather like him, but she was definitely holding something back. When he took her home she wouldn't let him see her to the door. He noticed she'd been right about the garden, at least from what he could see at the front. There was a muddy patch where she parked her old car, an equally muddy path and a few very neglected and untidy shrubs. There was a fuchsia in there he could see. If pruned back now it would give a cheerful show of flowers in autumn and the variegated euonymus needed attention or the plain green shoots would take over the whole bush.

"I did mean it about helping with the garden if you like."

"Can I let you know?"

He was hopeful; that's what she'd said about going out with him, but her worried face saddened him.

He went straight to his friends' home and asked, "Have I lost her?"

"No, you idiot. I wish I could bottle some confidence and tip it down your throat," Tony said. "You're nowhere near as bad looking as you think you are and listening to her you're damned near perfect."

"He's right," Louise added. "You say you're gangly, Petra

considers you tall and slim. Which you are. It's not just that though. You're steady and reliable, she's had experience of men who aren't. Look, talk to her and maybe mention how much you'd like a family."

"No way! I scared her off suggesting I tidy the garden. Suggesting setting up home together and raising a family would send her running."

"Aaaargh! You two!" Tony said.

Clearly there was something Ryan was missing.

Petra called him the following day. "Louise said we should talk. I think she's right. Do you want to come round on Saturday?"

He did and took a huge pink and white bunch of tulips, peonies and sweet Williams with him.

When she opened the door two cute little girls stood either side of her. Before he could even wonder what they were doing there, Petra introduced them as her twin daughters, Georgina and Lucia. He saw then that Louise had been right in thinking Petra wouldn't be scared off by a man who wanted a family. He said hello to the girls. They giggled as he reached down to shake their hands.

"You're Mummy's boyfriend, aren't you?" Lucia asked.

"Shhh. We talked about that remember," Petra said.

"You said he was just a friend but he brought you flowers like a boyfriend," Georgina pointed out.

"You are aren't you?" Lucia demanded.

Clearly the girls had none of their mother's shyness.

Trying to match their confidence Ryan nodded to admit being a boyfriend.

"Let me see your eyes then. Mummy said they're like chocolate."

Blushing, he knelt down and they stared into an eyeball each.

"I'd rather have real chocolate."

It was on the tip of his tongue to offer to buy them some, but he stopped just in time. Buying the children's affection wasn't the way, especially if he hoped to become more than an occasional visitor.

"How about you earn some by helping me sort out your garden?"

He kept them busy collecting up the prunings and grass cuttings and helping dig out weeds. It was even more fun than he'd imagined. The twins loved helping and learning plant names and Petra seemed really impressed with his skills and knowledge.

"I'm just going in for a bit," she said eventually. "The door's open so just yell if anyone needs me."

"Lunch is ready," she said when she reappeared.

Ryan hadn't realised it was that time, but a glance at his watch showed it was actually nearly two. He followed the others back into the house, expecting to leave, but saw the kitchen table had been set for all four of them. It felt so right eating together and the Spanish omelette was delicious. The treacle tart and custard were even better. He could get used to living like that, but he expressed his pleasure in less presumptuous terms. During the meal the girls kept up a stream of random questions about his job, blue whales, flowers and something he'd never heard of which might have been a TV programme. The meal took quite a long time.

The girls wanted to continue gardening in the afternoon.

"Can we grow flowers like the ones Ryan brought?"

Petra said, "I suppose we could buy some from the garden centre. Maybe you could suggest what to get, Ryan?"

"He can come with us, Mum."

"Ryan might have things to do this afternoon."

Was she tactfully telling him it was time to go? Or was Louise right and Petra was feeling as insecure as he did and therefore doubted he'd want to hang around any longer. One way to find out.

"You could buy plants with flowers already. That's not the only way though. I have some spare baby plants at the allotment, or ones we could take cuttings from and I have seeds. Would you like to plant those?"

He was interrupted to explain about cuttings, but spared any birds and bees type questions. "Growing from seeds and the rest means it takes longer to get flowers, but you'd really be growing them not just buying them."

"And you'll help us do it all, Ryan?"

"Yes, if you and Mummy want me to."

"Girls, why don't you go and draw a plan of how we'd like the garden to look and then Ryan can tell us which plants we need."

Excitedly they rushed off to do that.

"Ryan, before I lose my nerve... I don't want you to feel obligated or anything, but if Louise is right and you do really like me and you really are willing to keep coming back and help with the garden and everything then I'd like that very much indeed. I don't want the girls to get hurt though, or myself. If we start a garden, well it has to be more than that."

Seeing how hard it was for her to say that, he took her hand and gently squeezed it. "I understand, I think. I want to promise to stick around, but before I do there's something I have to ask. Tony said there was something about you he'd promised not to tell me..."

"But you know about that now."

"No."

"Georgina and Lucia."

"That's the worst there is to know?"

"Yes. I mean the fact I have two children, not that they're awful or I don't love them or anything. It's just the thought of a ready-made family scares some people and..."

"I want a family, very much. Not a ready-made one though."

She looked ready to cry.

"Families have to grow just like plants in gardens. I would like to be part of this one. I know I can't become their dad overnight, just as if we bought a tray of flowering pot plants and put them in the garden now – it'd look pretty for a few weeks but wouldn't last. To make a good job of it, something that'll get better year on year, we need to prepare the ground and work out which plants fit where and find out which ones everyone likes best."

"Yes, I see. So you want to put in a few cuttings, sow a few seeds and work from there?"

"Yes."

They were kissing when Lucia returned to ask, "What are

you doing?"

"Wondering what the garden will look like after we've done more work," Petra said.

"It'll look like this," Georgina said. She handed over their picture.

It was a riot of vibrant flowers around the edge and in the centre were the four of them. The adults were kissing and each held the hand of a child.

"That looks perfect," Petra said.

"Certainly does," Ryan agreed. "Come on then, let's go down the allotment and make a start."

5 A Brave Face

Iris put her name down for the allotments the day her parents said they were selling the family home. The small patch of ground wouldn't be as good as the huge garden back home, with its ancient apple trees and kitchen garden, but it would be better than nothing. That was the Adkins way; put on a brave face and make the most of things.

"You don't mind, do you? Us coming and living near you?" her mum said. "I promise we won't be in your pockets all the time."

"Of course I don't mind. It'll be great to see more of you." That was true.

Her dad explained the big place would soon be getting a bit much for them to maintain and was costly to run.

"Makes sense to move now, so we don't have to rush into buying and will be young enough to get settled into a new place. We'll have spare cash too. We'll treat ourselves to a few holidays and there'll be money for you too."

"Thanks, Dad. That's kind but I don't need it."

She didn't, nor did she want her parents thinking they'd had to bribe her into accepting their plans. What they'd said made perfect sense. Something was wrong though. Her parents were putting on a brave face. Over the years they'd got very good at that, but Iris sensed neither of them were truly happy. Iris wanted to tell them to snap out of it, admit their worries and talk to each other. She couldn't and even if she could, they wouldn't; it wasn't the Adkins way.

It took her parents a long time to find the perfect new home and sell the old one. Her parents put on a brave face throughout the entire process. The only time Iris thought she saw real emotion was when she asked her dad for the gardening tools he'd no longer be needing.

"Of course you can have them, love. Be nice to know they're still being useful."

She couldn't tell if he was pleased she intended to take up his favourite hobby or sad that he'd be giving it up.

Eventually the sale went through in midwinter. Iris went round to see how well her parents' furniture fitted into the new place and hear their plans for decorating.

They were still putting on a brave face. Although it wasn't the Adkins way, she challenged them. When they explained about the operation her mum needed she wished she hadn't.

"That's why you sold the house?"

"Yes," her dad agreed. "We weren't sure your mum would get better..."

He couldn't continue, but he didn't have to. Iris understood. She hugged them both and smiled bravely.

Her dad continued. "The operation is good news really. If it's successful..."

Iris heard she'd got her allotment plot shortly after her mum came out of hospital. Conveniently, it was between Iris's flat and her parents' bungalow. They could all walk down and meet there if they wished. As soon as she'd taken possession she went to tell her parents.

31

"I have a shed, so I could keep folding chairs there and maybe a camping stove to make tea."

"Nice idea," her dad said. "Let's go and take a look."

"There's nothing much to see," Iris protested, but they soon talked her into it.

"It's a good size," her dad said. He bent down and crumbled some soil in his fingers. "Excellent! Whoever had this before looked after it well. We'll soon have this producing all kinds of things... I mean you will."

"No, Dad. We will. I'm appointing you head gardener."

Iris's mum was impressed by the strawberry beds already in place. "You'll get a good crop off them, I shouldn't wonder. Maybe even enough for a few pots of jam?"

"I think you're right, Mum. I plan to grow tomatoes too, so maybe you could make a batch of chutney?"

Her mum beamed. Her main interest in the old garden had been picking flowers for arranging and gathering produce to cook with.

"I'm planning a couple of rows of flowers to attract useful insects. I might be able to spare you a few blooms."

"You're a good girl, Iris." Her mum had a tear in her eye, but the others pretended not to notice.

"Enough of that girly stuff," her dad said. "Let's be having a look at this shed of yours."

His tools were already in pride of place, but there was room for them to all squeeze in. It wasn't as smart as the summerhouse they'd once used for picnics, but Iris was sure they'd enjoy making use of it without having to put on a brave face.

6   What Lies Underneath

Shirley looked round at the bare earth. To her it looked like a battleground, but Hugh saw how beautiful the garden would be come spring.

"The daffodils and crocus we planted last month are making new roots below the ground. And can't you imagine the wallflowers and forget-me-nots when they're in full bloom?"

She couldn't. Oh, she was sure her friend was right and they'd look lovely in a few months, but at the moment the plants, transplanted from the nursery rows, looked very sorry for themselves.

Today she was helping him plant tulip bulbs. Shirley could see they had a quiet beauty to them, beyond the promise of the flamboyance to come. The smooth mahogany skins glowed in the autumn sun. She quite understood why in the past they'd been exchanged for huge sums of money by people who'd never see them bloom. But once buried in the soil they were gone from sight.

"We've done pretty well," Hugh said. "Thank you for your help once again."

"Come off it, we both know I'd rather be round here sharing your garden than stuck in my flat watching the telly."

Hugh sank to his knees before her and held out his hand.

At first she thought he was showing her that she'd missed planting a bulb. She stared at the thing in his hand which sparkled like a raindrop on a petal.

"I want you to share more than the garden. Will you marry me?" he asked.

"I can't. You know I can't."

"I know no such thing. You've said before you're not the marrying kind, but you've never given me a reason. Just hinted at some dark secret."

"I'm not the person you think I am."

"Then let me get to know the person you really are. Maybe I'll love her too."

Shirley just shook her head. "Shall I make tea while you put the tools away?"

"Right you are."

She let herself into Spring Cottage. Hugh moved there eight years ago, after the death of his wife, Cath. He and Shirley had become friends almost immediately after meeting in the village shop. She was there buying carrots and his purchase was of carrot seeds. Soon she'd learned they were both living alone, both childless.

"I miss Cath of course, I was lucky in my marriage. So many happy memories, but never the gift of a child."

She'd nodded as though she understood, as though her own experience hadn't been so very different. She'd never been married, but she'd had the gift he'd been denied and thought it a burden; one she'd given up quite willingly. Shirley got pregnant by mistake. She'd been just a child herself and terrified when she learned the truth. Her parents had easily persuaded her to have it adopted. The baby, she'd been told, was taken by people who loved and wanted him. She was free to get on with her life. She almost forgot about him until she was in her thirties and met someone who wanted to marry her and have a family. She knew it wasn't for her.

Somehow over the years she'd convinced herself that as she'd not loved the child, she didn't deserve to be loved. She'd kept what she'd done to herself and pushed people away. That wouldn't happen with Hugh. She might lose his friendship if she told him the truth, but she couldn't keep the truth buried any longer.

He listened quietly as, over a pot of tea, she explained as best as she could.

Hugh took her hand in his. "I understand..."

"I don't. I don't know how I could have done that." Tears fell, only a few and she soon had herself under control, but they brought some relief.

"Did you know that Spring Cottage isn't named for the season, but for the kind of spring which brings water?" Hugh asked.

"No." Grateful for the change of subject Shirley looked up and tried to smile encouragingly.

"Chap in the garden centre told me when I bought the bulbs." Hugh laughed. "Of course he waited until I'd paid in case it put me off buying so many."

"It didn't though?"

"No, but it did make me look at the deeds. Wait a minute, I'll show you." He brought photocopies and placed them on the table. "It's piped in now, but it came up right in front of the bank we've just planted. Be lovely to have a water feature here, don't you think?"

"If you mean a pond, then yes I think it would."

Hugh confirmed that was what he meant. "A good deep pond. We might get frogs if we're lucky and it'd be nice to see the flowers reflected in it. We'd get twice the value from them! And next to it a bog garden with lush hostas and primulas, and dragonflies darting overhead."

Shirley watched Hugh's face and knew he was already picturing the finished project. She'd noticed the 'we', so it seemed she'd get to see it herself when it was done. Although willing to help, she wasn't sure that they'd make much progress with the excavation.

"We can't do all that ourselves though. We'd need someone young and strong to do the work," she said.

"My nephew might be persuaded to help."

"That's a good idea." She'd met Neil a couple of times. He was a nice lad and had cheerfully tackled the task of clearing brambles from the bank and sawing through thick stems to cut back the unruly boundary fence. "Tell him I'll bake whatever he likes in the way of cakes."

When Neil arrived he brought with him a recipe book for cakes, pies and cookies. "I've marked the ones I like." Almost every page had a slip of paper in it. The recipe for lemon drizzle cake was highlighted in orange pen and had three markers, each with stars drawn on.

Shirley took the hint and made that, along with shortbread, a Victoria sandwich and tray of flapjack. Neil made good progress with the digging and short work of a large portion of her culinary offerings. The three of them discussed the work which they'd done and planned the next steps. Neil was almost as enthusiastic as Hugh, suggesting a pebbled beach area for birds to bathe and drink, and plants with coloured stems for winter.

"Yes, yes. It's going to be wonderful," Hugh said as he scribbled down notes.

Shirley smiled as they batted ideas back and forth. They were so alike in personality, though not in looks. Neil also shared his uncle's love of lemon drizzle cake. "Must be hereditary," she said as the two men cut the remains in half and took a piece each.

"No. It's not that, just coincidence," Neil said.

Coincidence? Then they weren't related. The boy must be adopted. As far as Shirley knew, she'd not met anyone who had been. He was clearly a happy, well-adjusted young man.

When Neil had gone she said to Hugh, "I see he's happy with his new family, but that doesn't make what I did right."

He looked confused. "Who?"

"Neil. He's not really your nephew is he? Not a blood relation?"

"He's Cath's brother's boy, so no not a blood relative but no less my real nephew because of it."

"Oh. Oh I see. I thought..."

"What did you think, Shirley?"

"That he was adopted. I thought you'd got him to reveal that and show me adopted people can be happy. I know they can, but that doesn't make what I did right."

"Neither does it mean you were wrong." He pulled her into a hug. "Do you want to talk?"

She almost said no, but realised it wasn't true. "I hoped my son would try to trace me when he turned eighteen, but that never happened. I wanted to know he was happy and that he forgave me. Guess he didn't?"

"Or for some reason didn't know he was adopted, or couldn't trace you, or thought it would be better not to."

"Maybe." She was quiet for a minute or two, then said, "I could have fed him, housed him..."

"Could you have really? Some young women do, they cope on their own and are good mothers. I don't know how they do, but some manage it. Many more struggle, are miserable themselves and cause problems for their children. Sometimes loving the child and doing their best aren't enough."

"You really think so?"

"I know. My mother wasn't married when I was born. She did her best, but it was hard on her, hard on us both. I know she resented me at times for the sacrifices she had to make for me."

"You don't know that."

"I do. She told me, not then but before she died she said she was sorry I'd had such a difficult childhood. We lived in hostels, relied on charity. We were never settled, never felt safe. It got better when I was at school and she could work. There were some good times, but she felt guilty always that she'd kept me with her and not given me up to someone who could give me a better life."

Shirley wasn't persuaded by this to believe she'd made the right decision, but gradually she came to see that perhaps there had been no right decision and she'd done the best she could, just as Hugh's mother had. Things were different now, she knew. There was more help for single mothers. More help too for people like her. She visited her doctor who referred her to someone she could talk to and that too helped.

"Did you forgive your mother?" she asked Hugh a few weeks later.

"Forgive her? I'm not sure I ever blamed her. I certainly don't now."

"So you didn't tell her that you understood and forgave her because you never thought there was anything to forgive?"

"That's right. Oh, I see... Yes that could be the case with your boy. You left a letter you said, explaining. Maybe he felt that settled the matter?"

That could be the case. It seemed now she'd never know, but she also knew it was in the past and not something she could change. She could only hope that, whether or not her son had a happy childhood, whether or not he felt bitter or betrayed at being abandoned, that he was happy now and wouldn't begrudge her the same.

Spring seemed to come in a warm colourful rush of flowers and new growth reflected in the water from the new spring-fed pond.

"You've seen it like this all along, haven't you?" she asked Hugh.

"Yes, I suppose so, right from when I first saw the cottage and misunderstood about the name. We know the truth now, so I think it should be a year round garden."

"What do you have in mind?"

"I'll show you." He did his best by walking her around the space, scratching in the earth where they'd create flower beds and placing sticks to represent roses and evergreen shrubs.

They planted lily bulbs and scattered seeds of brilliant blue cornflowers, feathery white ammi major, romantically named love-in-the-mist and cupid's dart. Hugh raked the soil level when they'd finished and they both stood back to look at the result. There wasn't really anything to see.

Hugh sank to his knees before her and held out his hand. At first she thought they'd dropped a seed packet. She stared at the thing in his hand which sparkled like a raindrop on a petal.

"Will you marry me?" he asked.

"Yes."

As he slid the ring on to her finger, Shirley looked again at the garden and saw not the fading tulips and bare earth, but the promise of what was to come. In her imagination, the flowers bloomed in shades of white and pink and blue. They'd be enough, she was sure, to pick for a wedding bouquet.

7   A Rainbow Life

My phone rang just as my youngest child managed to splatter my blouse with blackcurrant yoghurt. I dabbed at the stain as I checked to see who was calling. It was Ailsa. I should have guessed really as, out of all the people I know, Ailsa's the one who wouldn't understand what it was like getting two small kids ready for school. Ailsa doesn't do families. Ailsa does elegant, calm, quiet.

"Lou! I'm glad I caught you before you took the little ones to school."

She knows I'd never answer the phone while driving them anywhere.

I couldn't help picturing the horror that would show on her face if her peach coloured blouse were contaminated with food of such an uncomplementary shade. If Ailsa were in my position, which she never will be, the children would have been eating apricot yoghurt, or mango. Something that co-ordinated with her outfit. Her food-free clothes would be crisply ironed and her make-up perfect.

"Yeah, still here," I admitted, wishing that Ailsa's calmness would transmit itself to the kids so they'd eat without squabbling.

"I was wondering if you could pop round, on your way home, to see me... and meet my new goldfish."

Any comment I might have made to that was cut short by

the sight of my youngest attempting to balance orange juice on his head.

"Sure, see you soon," I said once tragedy was averted.

"Get your bags ready and your coats on," I told the kids. "If you're ready to go by the time I'm back you can have crisps with your lunch." In my opinion judicious bribery is the secret to successful parenting. I ran upstairs to change into something that was at least clean, even if it was a long way short of Ailsa's elegance.

Once the kids were safely delivered to school I drove round to Ailsa's house. She sounded as though something might be up. It wouldn't be much. Ailsa's life is pretty much all blue sky. Mine, in comparison, is rather stormy. I'm not jealous, far from it. There are rainbows in my world as well as wind and rain. Ailsa's avoidance of chaos and disorder mean she's missing out on a lot. An hour's peace at the end of my day to snuggle up with my husband is bliss, but I wouldn't swap the kids' noisy demands for day after day of quiet.

It wasn't until I stepped out the car that it occurred to me that, if she'd had her new pet more than a couple of days, my pink dress would clash with Ailsa's decor. Goldfish are orange, which means that whichever room it resided in would also be orange, or a complementary colour. They'd be a bowl of oranges artfully placed nearby to 'pick up' the colour. If it was in her study the bookcase would hold a few new volumes, all with orange covers. If the fish was in her living room the scatter cushions would match its scales perfectly. If in the dining room there'd be a bunch of tulips in the exact shade arranged nearby.

There was nothing I could do about my appearance other than to make the best of it, so I scrabbled in my bag for lipstick. I was in luck; the first one I found was almost exactly the right kind of pink. With the aid of my wing mirror I applied a generous smear and tidied my hair.

"You look nice," Ailsa said. Not even a mention that my bag and coat were very much the wrong shade of blue to complement the dress.

"Really?"

She held her hand out for my coat and hung it up. Ailsa looked me up and down and said, "Yes, really. That colour suits you."

"Thanks. And the coat?"

"Also quite nice, although possibly the combination of the two isn't the best."

"Oh good, you're not ill then."

She gave the kind of smile that said she acknowledged my sarcasm but was rising above it.

The moment I stepped into her living room, I thought I'd spoken too soon.

The walls had indeed been repainted; beige. The scatter cushions were replaced; with beige ones. A bowl of fruit was indeed artfully placed on the coffee table. It held Asian pears, nice to eat but not that exciting to look at because they're beige.

Maybe her fish was an albino and therefore beige? I looked round for the tank which I found in a shaded alcove. The lack of light didn't disguise the fact that the fish was bright orange.

"So you've got a goldfish."

"I did tell you."

"Yes, but it sounded unlikely somehow."

"It shouldn't as it was your idea."

"Mine?"

"You keep nagging me that I live alone in a fashion magazine and I should get into the real world and get myself some company."

Maybe I hadn't been quite as subtle as I'd thought. "I did not say that! Well, not exactly. Anyway, I was thinking of a family or at least a cat."

"I know. You remember Lily?"

"Who could forget?" She's Ailsa's niece and goddaughter. Ailsa loves her more than she loves her colour wheel. Lily is easy to love and very, very colourful. When she was tiny everything had to be bright, shocking pink. That was the nearest she came to sharing her aunt's colour sense. Lily got brighter and brighter. Her hair has been more colours than you'd find on a B&Q paint chart. The time before last that I saw her, one entire arm was covered in rainbow mermaids. I wasn't sure if the tattoos were real or not. The next time she was covered in tartan and chains. If I'd not known what a sweet, shy kid she really is I'd have been rather alarmed to be near the six foot punk.

"She's coming to stay."

"That's fantastic."

Nothing cheers Ailsa up like a visit from Lily and it reassures me she's not entirely missing out on family life.

"That's what I thought."

"But now you don't?"

"Yes, mostly. It's me I'm not feeling good about. I'm not always tactful when it comes to people's appearance, am I?"

"No."

"Thanks."

"Sorry, but it's true."

"Actually I meant it. I need to speak to someone who'll tell me the truth. Can I do this?"

"I don't see the problem. Lily's visited dozens of times and you've never upset her." I couldn't imagine Ailsa ever saying anything to hurt the girl.

"Remember when we sat in the garden last summer, drinking Brandy Alexanders?"

"Yes. They were the exact colour of the cushions on your patio furniture."

"Perfect, weren't they? And do you remember the butterflies?"

"Gosh yes. Hordes of red admirals appeared from nowhere and almost smothered that buddleja bush on the corner."

"Almost covered, yes. They clashed horribly with the lilac flowers, but we didn't mind that."

"Of course not."

"Pretty as they were, could you imagine me planting a rose bush that flowered in the same bright red as we saw on their wings."

Now I thought about it the butterflies were the only part of Ailsa's garden that wasn't in tasteful pastel shades. Even I'd been wearing cream that day.

"Not without also replacing every other plant."

"Lily's not just popping in for a few days. It's a kind of trial, ready for when she starts uni. Other than staying with me and family holidays she's not been away from home and is getting really nervous about living in halls."

I was beginning to understand.

"The plan is that she'll set up a bolt-hole in my spare room. Knowing she can jump in a taxi and be here in ten minutes might give her the confidence to cope. I know she looks confident but she's actually quite shy."

I nodded. I had guessed Lily might be sensitive under her bright exterior. In fact it seemed likely that shyness was the reason for the bright exterior.

"She's having a real crisis of confidence right now, apparently, and is very touchy about everything, including her appearance. If I say the wrong thing and upset her she might not go to uni. One word from me could wreck her entire life."

"Right." She was maybe being overly dramatic, but I saw her point. "That's why you've painted your living room in such a drab shade; Lily won't clash with it!"

"Exactly. Do you think it will work?"

I thought it might. If Ailsa could see her home as the background for a bright Lily-shaped butterfly, the girl's appearance shouldn't worry her. "I do. And that's why you were nice about my pink dress. Practising?"

"Partly, but it does suit you. I only ever mention what I don't like, don't I?"

"Yes."

"Thanks."

That time I knew she meant it. Luckily Ailsa and I are about the same size, so to desensitise my friend, I tried on items of her clothing, mixing and matching in more of a Lily than an Ailsa fashion. I reminded her she liked the items individually and encouraged her to try to think positively about them together. She did pretty well, considering.

"You'll do OK," I eventually decided. "You needn't actually keep praising her clothes, just refrain from being negative."

I didn't see Ailsa or Lily during her trial week, but I got a call just after the girl left.

"Please come round, Lou. I need you!"

I got there as quickly as I could. I didn't even stop to change my bright red shorts and yellow flowered top I'd been wearing to water my garden. I figured Ailsa would have seen so much colour the last few days that she'd hardly notice what I was wearing.

The front of Ailsa's terraced house looked just the same. The plants she had there were all white and silver and her front door was white so whatever the neighbours did, it could never clash. Inside was different though. The once golden hallway was now beige, if possible even duller than the one she'd used for the living room. The kitchen walls were slightly more cheerful, but still a version of beige.

"Well, am I pleased to see you!" she said.

"Didn't Lily's visit go well?" I asked as gently as I could.

"Brilliantly! She's gone home to get more of her stuff and says I've made her feel much more confident about starting uni."

"That's great. So why do you need me?"

"I want your advice with the redecorating."

"Mine?"

"Yes. It's all so dull isn't it?"

"Well, yes," I answered in the same tone she'd previously used to comment on some of my colour combinations.

"I need to brighten it up! I've just realised that I'm so keen on good colour combinations because I love colour."

"With Lily moving in, you'll have plenty."

Ailsa shook her head and pointed to the only none beige thing, other than the fish, in the room. It was a black cushion. "That's Lily's." She beckoned me upstairs where Lily had already put her quilt cover on the bed. It was black. On the dressing table I saw bottles of black nail varnish

"She's become a Goth," Ailsa said just as I was beginning to guess that. "All her clothes are black, her make-up, accessories, everything."

"Which is good, surely? Black is classic and goes with everything." I said that in my best attempt at Ailsa's accent.

"It does, even beige. But I don't want a beige life. It's time to add some colour and I'm not just talking about paint. We've decided Lily will live here rather than go into halls."

I knew her calm life was about to get stormy. I knew too that when she saw the rainbows she wouldn't regret her decision.

8 Letters To A Magazine

Dear Agony Aunt

I'm a terrible person. Terrible mother because I'm never there for my kids, I foist them off on other people too often. They have to eat school dinners because I don't have time to make them a decent lunch. They walk to school because I'm not there to drive them. They have to do a lot of things for themselves because I'm not around enough.

I'm a terrible employee and colleague because I barely have time for other staff. I don't socialise with them. I can never do overtime or cover for people who want a day off. If there's an emergency and I have to stay late it gives others work, phoning my family, making sure my children are OK. I must look a mess too.

My friends must be fed up. I don't talk to them enough, be with them much. They'll get an occasional text if they're lucky and birthday gifts are usually the result of a last minute call to the florist.

My mother-in-law must feel so used. She needs support and instead I use her as an on-demand baby-sitter. Even neighbours are made use of to walk the dog and tend the garden.

Please help me to show all these people I really do care about them and that I'm so sorry I can't do more.

Yours in desperation, Mandy Reilly.

Dear Editor

I saw your offer to send flowers to someone who deserves it. I'd like to nominate our family doctor, Dr Reilly. She's brilliant. Never judgemental if my kids have an accident. She's a working mother herself she tells me and knows it just isn't possible to spend every second of every day wrapping them in cotton wool.

She never makes me feel I'm wasting her time and I always leave the surgery feeling better than when I went in, no matter how ill I am. Her kindness truly is the best medicine.

Yours faithfully,

Alison Davies.

Dear Beauty Editor

How can I look as good as my colleague? (picture enclosed)

She's got the confidence to go without make-up and usually her gorgeous hair is just pulled into a ponytail – yet she looks better than I do after hours in the bathroom.

I'm a doctor, so know a healthy diet and lifestyle are important for looking good and I do try, but I just can't recreate the glow she has. Mandy's a great person, please don't tell me that her being beautiful on the inside is the secret to looking good on the outside as I could never match her kindness, patience, encouragement... well the list goes on.

Tanye Chabbria

Dear nice lady in the magazine,

You sometimes do pictures and writing of people who are really nice and you give them presents and stuff. Could you do that for our Mum as she's the bestest really nice person ever.

Mum works really hard making people all better course she is a doctor. She makes us not be ill too. When she is at work we go to school. If we are not at school she lets us go to our grannys house or go out places with our uncle Gerald. Granny and uncle Gerald are really nice to, but Mum is even nicerer.

Love from Jacob and Amanda Reilly.

Dear Gardening Editor,

I have a wonderful neighbour who's made such a difference to my life. I suffered from depression, which she treated me for. (She's my GP.) The medical treatment was helpful, but her friendship even more so. As you surely realise, gardening is a great therapy. I don't have any outdoor space myself other than a window box, but Dr Reilly allows me to tend her garden whenever I wish.

I'd like to buy a small tree as a thank you and wondered what you'd suggest for a medium sized, sunny garden on clay soil? My friend has a dog and two children, but both are very well behaved! I think some form of fruit tree might be appreciated.

Yours truly

George Wednesday.

Dear Picture Desk,

I thought you'd like to see this snap of my friend Mandy and me at the seaside. As you can see, I've buried her in the sand, with help from her kids. It's the only way to stop her rushing off and doing things for other people!

She's amazing. Brilliant at her job, fantastic mother and the best friend ever. We both have busy lives so don't spend as much time together as we'd like, but I treasure every minute!

Best wishes,

Serena Beech.

Dear Jacob and Amanda Reilly,

Thank you so much for writing to us about your lovely mum. Lots of other people have too, including your granny and the lady who walks your dog Dewdrop, when you're at school. I think giving your mum presents and taking her photograph and writing about her in the magazine is a very good idea. Thank you for thinking of it.

I have spoken to some of your mum's friends and we've made a plan. We want it to be a surprise though, so please don't tell her yet! (That's why I've sent this letter to your granny's address.)

What we have arranged is that Dr Tanye Chhabria will ask your mum to come with her to our offices, because she's getting a makeover and wants a friend to go with her. When your mum gets here it will really be her who has the hair cut, new clothes and everything. Afterwards we'll take her for a lovely meal with her friends, your granny and most importantly you two!

Afterwards she will be given flowers and a plum tree and other presents. I do hope you think she will like all this. Remember to keep it a surprise.

I look forward to meeting you both on the day.

With very best wishes,

The Editor.

9   The First Time I Saw Jasmine

The first time I saw Jasmine she was being carried. Nothing odd about that; we were both babies. It feels like I've always known Jasmine and everything about her. No, it's more than that. Destiny or something. Oliver Spring melting the heart of Jasmine January, that's how it's supposed to be.

As befits her three months' seniority, Jasmine could talk before me. Walk before me. I followed in her wake.

The first time I heard Jasmine, she was screaming. Nothing odd about that if you knew Jasmine. She felt things deeply.

Me too, but I'm quiet.

Then Jasmine saw me and her screams turned to delighted squeals. That's what I remember; having the power to make her happy just by my presence. She did the same to me.

"I'll help you," she often said. Shoe-lace tying and crayon holding were mastered by copying her.

Jasmine ran ahead but always looked back to see if I was following.

"Come on, Ollie," she'd yell. If I dropped back she'd wait and let me catch up.

Following the pattern, Jasmine was the first in our class to kiss, get drunk, be expelled. That last one was because of drugs. It was the first time she broke my heart. I was jealous about the kissing, but her attempts at self destruction hurt more.

She was still ahead of me. Seeing where she was headed I didn't want either of us to go there.

"Come on, Jasmine," I coaxed her back.

I studied for my exams, started work, moved on. I didn't look back to see if Jasmine was following because it seemed she'd raced ahead again.

Months later I saw her carried out of a club, too drunk to stand. She was abandoned on the pavement. I took her home. In the morning we talked.

"You're on a downward spiral, Jasmine. You have to stop before it's too late."

"Already is, Oliver." She showed me the scars on her arm.

"I'll help you," I said.

"No one can."

"I'll help you."

"I've done bad things."

"I'll help you." I wanted to tell her I loved her, but she wasn't ready to hear it. She had to learn to love herself before she'd believe anyone else did.

Most of my help consisted of offering a shoulder to lean or cry on. She did both. For once I lea her; to professionals who really could help. During the first few visits I stayed by her side and held her hand. Gradually she learned to trust them and got stronger.

I changed my hours at work so we could walk together through the woods every day over the autumn and winter. Christmas and New Year slipped quietly by. Gradually Jasmine pulled herself out of the darkness.

It snowed and we threw snowballs and built a snowman just as we had when we were kids. My cold hands couldn't tie the scarf around his neck.

"I'll help you." Jasmine took my fingers between hers to warm them.

It rained and we walked close together under an umbrella.

Wintery sun sparkled on the frost-coated branches of the trees lining the path. Jasmine ran on ahead. She looked back and called, "Come on, Ollie."

Jasmine found a patch of snowdrops. "I didn't know these were here," she said.

"They're always there, under the ground, waiting for a time when they can be appreciated."

"Like you? You've always been there. You've known the worst of me and yet you love me."

I stepped closer, hoping to take her in my arms. "Yes."

It was no good, before I'd given my answer Jasmine ran on again. She stopped when a foot cracked through ice into muddy water.

"Isn't that always the way?" she asked. "I go on ahead into trouble."

I picked her up and carried her over the puddle. "And this will always be the way, Jasmine. I'll be right behind you, ready to pick you up if you need it."

"No, Oliver. That's not how it should be. Put me down."

Reluctantly I did as she asked.

"It's time for me to stop rushing ahead and walk by your side." She took my hand and did just that.

10 An Active Imagination

Rebecca ushered the customer into her office. "Do take a seat."

Before her bottom touched the cushion, the lady started speaking. "I don't understand how they got my details. I'm always very careful to shred my receipts and statements."

"We don't believe this is your fault," Rebecca assured her. "I just need to know which purchases you made yourself so the others can be investigated."

"Oh, yes I see. I know I used it in the garden centre."

Rebecca and the lady went through the account, item by item, confirming which were and which were not genuine sales. As they did so, Rebecca felt she was getting to know far more about the woman than she would have from dozens of conversations. She knew the shops she used, charities she supported and organisations she belonged to.

Rebecca wished she could tell her twin sister about the customer and the insight she'd gained into her life. She'd also liked to have discussed the large regular payments the lady made to a shop which specialised in making life-sized, realistic dolls. Why would she do that? She and Kelly could have come up with all sorts of improbable suggestions, she was sure. As the bank's strict policy of confidentiality meant Rebecca couldn't reveal any of the details to Kelly, she'd have to find something else to occupy her sister's mind.

Although Kelly was recovering well from the accident, she still rarely left her home and would always need the wheelchair. Maybe it was just as well Rebecca wasn't able to make her job sound too interesting. Kelly had been forced to give up hers as a police community support officer and it was likely to be some time before she'd be able to do any kind of work again. It wasn't surprising Kelly was bored.

Rebecca selected an armful of mysteries and thrillers from the library. Hopefully Kelly wouldn't have already read them all. Then she bought a selection of cakes and went to visit her sister.

Kelly must have been waiting for her, as she opened the door before Rebecca had got her key out of her bag.

"Oh good, you've brought cakes. I nearly rang and asked you to get something to go with cups of tea."

"Time for another shopping trip, is it?"

"Yes. I've got a new neighbour and she finished off all my biscuits."

"At last!" The huge house next to Kelly's end-of-terrace had been sold just after Christmas, but had been empty for the past three months. "What's she like, other than hungry?"

"I'd like to say that was just because of the moving in, but actually she's as wide as she is high so she probably does eat a fair bit. Once she saw I meant the offer of tea and things she was happy to accept. I've had a busy day keeping her and the removal men supplied with refreshments and being nosey about her furniture."

"I hope you're not too tired to make another cup for your dear sister?"

"I had a nap earlier and the thought of cake is reviving

me."

"Well, get the kettle on then and give me all the gossip."

Kelly made the drinks and then said, "Her name is Daisy Butler. She's travelled around quite a lot during her lifetime and now intends to settle down. That's all I know so far."

"No family?"

"None she mentioned, but we didn't talk much. She didn't mention working either, but I guess she did and is now retired."

They discussed the lady for some time. Kelly described her weird assortment of furniture and they guessed at the lady's history. As she apparently lived alone. Rebecca decided she'd been widowed tragically young and never got over it.

"No, she's never been married but had a string of lovers. Still has actually, lots of men have been visiting." Kelly gave a wicked grin.

"To unload her chairs and connect up her phone?"

"Could be that, I suppose," Kelly conceded.

Kelly looked more animated than she had for some time. Rebecca guessed the effort involved in making the drinks, and wheeling herself in and out the house to hand them over the fence, had done her some good and the thought of being useful had done even more.

On Rebecca's next visit Kelly reported that her new neighbour had brought round a bunch of tulips and mixed narcissi the following day as a thank you for the tea.

"She's really bright, in all senses of the word. She's got pink hair and a truly dazzling wardrobe. She's cheerful and seems intelligent. A touch scatty though. She often talks about random things as though I'll know what she means and she borrowed a cup of sugar and returned a bag of onions."

The following day a lady matching Kelly's description of Daisy, including an orange jacket over a purple skirt, came into the bank. After speaking to the cashier she emptied her enormous yellow handbag over the floor.

Rebeca discreetly asked the cashier if everything was all right.

"The lady is trying to pay in a cheque, but the paying in book she has with her is for a different account. She's trying to find another one, or something with the other account number on."

"OK. Buzz me if there's a problem." She retreated to her office without the customer noticing her. Having to go through the contents of her handbag would be quite embarrassing enough without extra witnesses.

Over the next few days, Rebecca heard that Daisy had asked for advice on things such as when the bins were emptied and who she could ask to come and help sort out her overgrown garden.

"I said I thought it looked rather romantic, with all the spring blossom. She agreed it did and we got talking about flowers. I told her I'd enjoyed arranging the flowers she gave me and she immediately went out and cut armfuls of blossom and greenery from her garden."

Daisy had also asked Kelly to come for walks with her, so she could get her bearings on the local area.

"She's like you in seeing that although my legs are useless, the rest of me still works," Kelly told her sister.

"Perhaps she's had experience of people with disability. Her fiancé might have been injured in the war and she nursed him until..." she trailed off. The only possibilities she wanted to raise with Kelly were optimistic ones.

"Until he recovered and they married? I'm not sure she's old enough for that. More likely she's just a sensible person. Kind too. She's got a spare key to this place and I have her number so I can ring her if I ever have a problem. She said she'd much rather be called at three in the morning than find out later I'd had a fall and had to wait hours for help."

A few days later though, Kelly reported something which suggested Daisy wasn't quite so sensible.

"She's got an imaginary friend," Kelly said

"It's not that odd," Rebecca said. "We had a whole castle full, didn't we?"

"Yes, but people usually grow out of it. We did. Daisy's just started and she must be well into her seventies."

"How do you know about it?"

"She's started talking to herself. Well, she talks to someone called Harold, but he isn't there and I've never seen her with a mobile. She seems to do it early mornings and evenings."

Kelly spent as much time outside as she could, so often wheeled herself on to her patio now the days were getting warmer. "I can see and hear her through the trellis fence, but she probably doesn't realise I'm there. During the day when people are about she either talks to them or keeps quiet."

"Let's go out and see if she's doing it now."

"She'd hear me open the French doors."

"True. Let's go out anyway and I can say hello if she's there and get a look at her."

As soon as they went out, Daisy called out a greeting to Kelly and raised her head above the overgrown fence. She was the person Rebecca had seen at the bank, but of course Daisy hadn't seen her so didn't recognise her.

Kelly conducted the introductions, exchanging an eye roll with Rebecca as Daisy remarked how alike they looked. The conversation then moved to the weather.

"The forecast on TV last night was completely wrong," Daisy said.

"It usually is. I prefer checking the meteorological reports online," Kelly said.

"On a computer? I don't have one of those and wouldn't know what to do with it if I had."

"I could show you."

"No thank you. I have enough trouble with the TV remote."

Then Kelly decided it was a bit cool for her and she and Rebecca went back inside.

"You recognised her didn't you? From work I suppose?" Kelly asked as soon as the door was shut.

"You know I can't say anything because of confidentiality. Fraudsters could use information like that. If they knew when she moved and which bank she was with they could send quite a plausible letter or email."

"I suppose so." Kelly grinned. "If she's not a customer I'll have to assume you've taken up pole dancing and she's your teacher."

"My pole dancing career is also confidential."

"Yeah, like you could keep a secret from me!"

Rebecca had to concede that was true. Thankfully she didn't have anything to hide.

"I was wondering," Kelly said. "If she's talking to a ghost. Maybe you were right about her loving someone and he died?"

"What sort of things does she say?"

"Are you there, Harold? What's the weather like? She tells him what it's like here and what's been in the news. Doesn't that suggest he could be 'on the other side'?" She spoke the last four words in a weird, wobbly voice.

"Not particularly."

A few days later, Kelly excitedly told her she'd found out the truth. "She was out this morning and the postman asked me to take in a parcel. It was addressed to Mr H. Butler."

"Harold?"

"Exactly. Her dead husband."

"People don't send parcels to dead people."

"Not if they know they're dead. Obviously she killed him and is pretending he's still alive. He must have done something awful to drive her to it as she's really sweet. I wonder if his body was in one of those boxes she brought here?"

"You really are letting your imagination run away with you. We need to find you a hobby or something."

"Actually, the doctor says he thinks I'm strong enough to consider working part-time now, if I can find something suitable."

"That's great news. I'll ask around."

She did, but there weren't many jobs on offer anywhere. The out of town supermarket had vacancies and as they were a huge company Rebecca assumed they must employ some wheelchair users. The store was quite a way from Kelly's home though and would require two separate bus journeys. The only other possibility was closer, but would mean Kelly negotiating her way across the same busy junction as she'd been on when she was knocked down.

Rebecca had texted Kelly several times but hadn't visited her for a week when she returned to the bank from her lunch break and saw Daisy leaving. It would have been impossible not to see her. She was wearing a dress the same bright pink as her hair and carrying her enormous yellow handbag. Rebecca said hello to her.

"Oh hello, dear."

"I'm glad to have seen you. I wanted to thank you for being so kind to Kelly." She thought, but didn't say, 'and see if you seem like a crazed murderer'.

"Just neighbourly is all. She's the same, takes in my post if I'm not there and has my spare key in case I lock myself out and her blue badge makes things so much easier for shopping trips. Mostly though she's just a joy to be around. I'd be lonely rattling around that house all on my own, without her to chat to sometimes."

Despite Daisy's flamboyant appearance she seemed perfectly normal and nice. It was easy enough to imagine her eccentric enough to talk to herself as she tended her garden, but impossible to imagine her as a killer.

Rebecca collected the contents of her colleagues' out trays

and took everything to the back office. As she worked through the paperwork she noticed a cheque made out to a Mr H. Butler had been deposited. Rebecca couldn't help wondering if it was connected with the mysterious Harold and the fact that Daisy seemed to conduct banking matters in two different names. There were plenty of perfectly legal reasons for paying money into someone else's account, but there were dishonest ones too. And there had been that parcel Kelly had taken in for Daisy. That was odd and... Daisy had access to Kelly's home at any time!

A quick search on her computer showed Rebecca that her sister's neighbour had an account in the name of Miss Daisy Butler and that there had been several large money transfers from Mr H. Butler's account going into it. The address for Mr Butler's account was the same as Daisy's, even though she'd just admitted she lived alone.

Remembering the customer whose debit card had been used fraudulently, Rebecca looked closely at Daisy's recent transactions. She had the usual payments for electricity, telephone and insurance. There wasn't anything to the company Kelly had reported seeing deliver a television, nor to the decorating firm, despite work having been completed. There were two payments to a men's clothing shop and a recently set up standing order to an internet provider. Daisy's clothes were peculiar, but not in any way manly and she'd made a point of telling them she couldn't use a computer.

Was Kelly in danger? Should she warn her to be wary of Daisy? Rebecca told herself that there was no proof Daisy had done anything wrong and that even if she had there would be no reason for her to harm Kelly. Even so she went to see Kelly straight after work.

"You OK, Sis?" Kelly asked.

"I'm fine. And you?"

"Good, yes. Just like always."

"And Daisy? Is she just like always? Still talking to Harold?"

"Yes. Well, no. She still talks to him, but it's not muttering stuff at night now. She talks to him in the day. Actually, she shouts. Yesterday she asked him if he'd make her a cup of tea and I thought she was talking to me and answered."

"Oh, you've seen him. That's a relief."

"No, actually I haven't. She says he won't come out as it's too cold."

"What? We're practically having a heatwave."

"Yes. He must be hiding," Kelly said.

"Or she is." Rebecca hesitated. She shouldn't discuss customers with someone who didn't work for the bank, but she and Kelly were identical twins, so really it was no different than telling herself. Plus, she had to warn Kelly. Rebecca told her sister everything she knew, which amounted to very little. She suspected a whole lot more.

"So what do you think?" Kelly asked. "There's a live Harold, a dead Harold or there never was a Harold?"

"Definitely one of those. Either she's stealing his money, or blackmailing him or made him up so she can launder money or… well there are lots of possibilities."

"Oh, I thought you meant he was a spy, or on a witness protection scheme or maybe a celebrity trying to avoid the press after a scandal."

"What? Get a grip."

"You think it's more likely that my four foot, seventy-year-old, pink haired neighbour is a serial killer?"

"Not a serial killer, no." Actually she still couldn't really picture Daisy as any kind of criminal. She'd given Kelly her key, which suggested she didn't have anything to hide. Kelly had only been in her neighbour's house a few times, but that was because to start with she didn't have a ramp to allow easy access for her chair. She asked the workmen who were refurbishing the house to make one, but of course the work they were doing meant that although Kelly could get in, there wasn't much space. Anyway, the unusually warm weather meant sitting in the garden was much more pleasant.

"Something is going on," Rebecca insisted, though not very forcefully.

"We could just ask her, instead of jumping to conclusions?"

"OK." Feeling silly, Rebecca insisted they have their phones switched on. She slipped a heavy crystal vase into her handbag to use as a weapon should Daisy attack them.

"Oh, hello girls!" Daisy said when she answered her door. "Have you come to see how the decorating looks?"

"I wondered what colours you'd chosen," Kelly said.

Maybe that was true. Daisy's dress sense was a source of wonder to Rebecca, so maybe Kelly had been thinking about her decor. Today she was wearing an orange T-shirt and turquoise… well on most women they'd have been shorts, but they didn't expose much of Daisy's legs.

"Come in, then and have a look round. Would you like a cold drink? We were just about to have one."

"We?" Rebecca asked as she looked round at the cream

hallway.

"Yes. Oh, of course you haven't met my brother Harold." She pointed them towards the lounge. "You say hello and I'll fetch those drinks."

The sisters moved slowly towards the room which was also cream and contained a man who looked rather like Daisy might if she'd been stretched. They stared at Harold who was reading a book and wearing an assortment of jumpers and scarves and a huge leather hat. After a moment, Kelly wheeled herself forward.

"Hi, I'm Kelly from next door and this is my sister, Rebecca." She extended a hand which Harold shook as he gave his name.

"Nice to meet you at last, Kelly," he said. "And you too, Rebecca."

Daisy appeared with a tray of bright and lavishly decorated cocktails. "What's up with you two? You look like you've seen a ghost."

Kelly made a strange noise. Rebecca looked at her sister, saw she was trying not to laugh and wished she hadn't. Soon they were both trying to stifle giggles. Trying and failing.

"I'm sorry," Rebecca said once they had themselves under control. "We weren't absolutely sure you were real, Harold."

"I heard you talking to him, Daisy but I never saw him and I thought you lived alone."

"I did!" Daisy chuckled. "It's a wonder you didn't think me batty."

"I'm sure they did, Daisy," Harold said.

Daisy fetched her tiny phone and hooked it on to her

glasses. With her hair it was impossible to see it.

"Harold stayed in Australia to sell our house there and sort out all the paperwork while I came over to buy this one."

"Ah! And you phoned him in the mornings or evenings because of the time difference?" Kelly said.

"That's right," Harold said. "Sorry about being such a recluse this week, but it's the end of summer in Australia now, so it seems really cold over here."

"Ah. Right."

"So did you think my dear sister had made me up, or that I was a ghost?"

Both Harold and Daisy looked so interested and amused that they confessed to their earliest guesses. The delighted reaction they received persuaded them to admit all their later suspicions too.

"Well you got one of them right, well nearly. Can you work out which one?" Harold asked.

"As you're alive and clearly on good terms with Daisy I don't think it can be anything to do with her," Kelly said. "So you're a spy, or in hiding for some reason?"

"Close enough. I was involved in the cold war. I want to write my life history, but as there are still things I can't reveal or which are sensitive, I'm going to have to fictionalise it. What I need is an assistant with an imagination like yours to help make it interesting. Don't suppose either of you girls can type and want a job?"

"Yes and yes," Kelly said.

11 The Scent Of Lilac

"Mum, what was Nan's full name?" As Flora spoke, a heavy perfume filled the room.

"Agatha Myrtle Galbraith. Why love?"

"If we're going to apologise we should get things right."

"Flora, are you sure you want to do this?"

"What can you smell?"

"Lilac."

"What can you hear?"

"Your sisters, crying."

"Then what choice do I have?"

"You're sure Nan is really haunting your sisters? Perhaps they're just frightened because they saw her die."

"She's been dead for almost a year and they're getting worse, not better. And the scent hasn't faded. It gets stronger each time she's mentioned, I'm sure that's why we've all got sore throats."

Rose helped her daughter find a brooch and shawl of Agatha's. As they handled the shawl, the scent increased.

Flora and her sisters walked to the village hall.

"Will Nan really be there?"

"Yes, Clover. Then you and Louise can apologise for frightening her. I'll say sorry too, because I think she's angry with all of us."

"Then she'll leave us alone?"

"I hope so."

Inside the hall, Flora marked out a five-pointed star. She placed a candle on every point, then ushered her sisters into place. Her grandmother's shawl and brooch were placed in the empty places. Flora lit each candle.

"Now we must all think about her."

"It won't really work will it?"

"Just saying sorry won't, but I'm going to call her back from the dead. Then we'll make her go away and stay away."

"That's not what you told Mum."

"She wouldn't let us do this if I'd told the whole truth."

"What if it doesn't work? Will Nan never leave us alone?" asked Louise.

"Are you going to do this? It won't work if we don't all do it."

"We will, Flora," chorused the younger girls.

"As I was saying, when she comes we'll tell her we're sorry."

They each thought of the dead woman. Flora remembered how her nan spread nasty rumours about her father, suggesting an unhealthy attachment to his daughters. She remembered too everything she'd heard of her mother's awful childhood.

The younger ones remembered their grandmother calling them close and then giving painful pinches. She said mean things about their mother and tried turning them against their sister.

Clover remembered too that afternoon, exactly a year ago. She had listened to her teacher talking about bullies.

"Bullies are really cowards," Miss had said. "You should always report them and, if you can, stand up to them. It sometimes frightens them off."

She told her sisters, who agreed their nan was a bully. Clover and Louise had decided to frighten her away. They hid in this same hall and waited for her to come for piano practice. They appeared under a sheet, wailing. She hadn't died of fright. She became angry. She'd screamed and chased them, walking stick raised. She fell down the steps, broke her neck and died. The family thought they'd lost the bully until the funeral. Agatha's angry presence was felt as fully in death as it had been in life. The sweet sickly scent was so strong the guests quickly left.

A year later, the sisters still smelled the lilac fragrance.

"Agatha Myrtle Galbraith, we call you to us. Agatha Myrtle Galbraith we call you to us," Flora whispered.

Her voice became louder each time she repeated the incantation. Her sisters joined in the chant. Slowly the shawl and brooch stirred and rose. The shawl draped as if supported by a body. The brooch hung as if pinned on to it. The candles flickered and dimmed.

The light regained its strength to reveal a figure wrapped in the shawl. It was faint, barely the shadow of a reflection. They recognised Agatha.

"Sorry we frightened you, Nan," said Louise.

"We didn't want you to die, just to see what it's like to be scared."

"They are sorry, Nan, and I'm sorry too. I should have known what they were planning and stopped them," Flora said.

The girls repeated their apologies and each in turn begged Agatha to leave them in peace. As they spoke the lilac scent increased. Through their streaming eyes, they saw the figure growing taller and stronger. Agatha was now more substantial than she'd been in life. She looked bright and strong. They screamed.

"I'm not sorry," shouted Rose from the doorway. "You were cruel to me and you were cruel to the children." Rose hugged the girls. "When Ralph died you said you wanted us to come home. I thought you'd changed. I was wrong. You just wanted to share your misery."

As Rose shouted, the figure began to spin, sending sparks and clouds of perfume at every turn. She became paler, smaller.

"Agatha Myrtle Galbraith, I called you to us, now we send you back. Agatha Myrtle Galbraith, we send you back," whispered Flora.

All four of them repeated the phrase. They barely whispered the words yet the air seemed full of their rhythm.

Agatha spun faster and faster. Then with a hiss, she cast off the shawl and flew about the hall wailing and thrashing. Lilac scent choked them and the unearthly sounds throbbed through their bodies.

Then silence. Agatha was gone.

They never smell Lilac now, not even in spring when the flowers bloom.

12 Bird Watching

Hayley clicked the remote to start the nature DVD again. Usually the gentle sound of wood pigeons cooing comforted her. Today it was making her cry, but crying was all she felt capable of. Silly really; there was nothing for her to be sad about now.

Pigeon had been her father's nickname for her when she was little. He and her mum had put a bird table where she could see it from her bedroom window and Hayley sprinkled seeds for the feathered visitors. Pigeons had been the first birds she'd learnt to recognise and so had always been her favourite. She couldn't remember if that's why her dad chose her nickname or if the name had been what prompted her interest in the pigeons.

When her gran had said, "Daddy and Mummy were hit by a car and have gone to heaven," Hayley had imagined them flying there on pale grey wings. She'd gone to live with her grandparents in the country. Hayley had been upset to leave the birds.

"We'll take your bird table and the birds will come and see you in your new home," her gran said.

They must have been different creatures to the ones she'd seen with her parents, but to the little girl she'd been, it seemed as though some were the same. She imagined they were sent to her new home by her parents, to look after her.

As Hayley grew, pigeons always brought comfort. She could hear them cooing as she sat her exams, they flew encouragingly past as she took her driving test and roosted on the sign of the shop where she worked.

She'd been throwing crusts for the pigeons the day she met Greg. He was a bird lover too. They often went to nature reserves together. Six months ago, they saw a kingfisher. Hayley had chattered about its beautiful plumage until Greg proposed, startling her into silence.

"Yes," she'd whispered.

A wood pigeon cooed gently as they kissed.

A month after that, Hayley guessed she was pregnant. Walking back from the doctor's after having this confirmed she'd heard pigeons again and known everything would be all right.

There had been no time to stop and listen for birds as the couple made plans to bring forward their wedding and get their love nest ready. On honeymoon, they'd listened to kookaburras laughing as though the birds shared their joy.

Greg's parents gave them a bird table as a housewarming present. Hayley had shed a few tears then, remembering the one from her childhood and the loss of her own parents.

"What's wrong, love?" her mother-in-law had asked.

"Nothing, it's a lovely thought." Hayley hugged the older woman and told her about the one her parents had bought so long ago.

They'd assembled the bird table and stocked it with seeds. No birds had come during the first week.

"It will take time, but they'll come," Greg's mother said.

She was right. Starlings soon found the table, as did sparrows and magpies. When three of those arrived together, Greg had wanted to buy pink paint for the nursery.

"Wait a bit, there might be four next week. We can't go re-painting every time I put out more seed," Hayley joked.

They hung strings of peanuts for blue tits and added a nyger feeder to attract finches. Greg tried to photograph each new species whenever he had the chance.

"Isn't it odd that we never seem to get any pigeons?" Hayley asked. She smiled brightly in an attempt to hide the sadness in her voice.

"They must come when we're at work," Greg assured her. "We don't have much time for watching at the moment. I expect there are all kinds that we don't see; perhaps even woodpeckers."

She knew he was right. She kept telling herself he was right as she lay awake beside him. In the morning, as she was sick again, she tried to imagine there were pigeons in the garden. It had been weeks since she'd had time to stop and look out the window before work; morning sickness didn't allow for that.

"Will you phone work for me, Greg? I'm going back to bed."

Hayley had slept for a while and then got up to look out the window. The only birds she saw were starlings and a single magpie. She'd put on the film of wood pigeons to try to cheer herself up. She was watching it for the second time when she heard the doorbell.

"I phoned you at work and was told you were off sick, so I just thought I'd pop round and make sure you were OK," her mother-in-law said.

Hayley opened the door wide and invited her in.

"Hayley, love, what on earth is the matter?"

"Just morning sickness really and I, oh I don't know, I just feel so sad."

"Hormones?"

"My parents will never see my baby," Hayley sobbed. It wasn't until she said it she realised how much that distressed her. "I've always thought they were close, watching over me somehow, but now it seems as though they've abandoned me, or I've abandoned them by getting married and having a new family."

"Oh, Hayley love, I don't know what to do. Would you like me to go?"

"No, please don't. Don't you leave me too."

"I won't, not if you don't want me to. I feel awkward with you; I'd like to be a mother to you, not that I think I could make up for your loss, but then I worry that might remind you of what you've missed..."

"It's OK; really. You just be you; my lovely mother-in-law."

They hugged and soon they were both crying.

"Look at the pair of us," Hayley said when she felt calmer. "You'd think my throat was sore enough from the morning sickness without me making it worse by crying and I don't know what your excuse is."

"The thought of becoming a grandmother has had a strange effect." She grinned at Hayley. "Shall we have a cup of tea and look at the baby clothes catalogue, I think that would help."

"Good idea, I'll put the kettle on."

As she made the tea, Hayley realised her sadness had disappeared.

"Thanks, Mum," she said, using the term for the first time as she squeezed her mother-in-law's shoulder. "You've really cheered me up."

"You make me happy too. Oooh, that reminds me about why I was trying to call you in the first place. As I came back from shopping this morning, I saw two wood pigeons perched on the roof of your house. I thought you'd like to know."

13 Peace Cottage

Richard left his car in the convenient off-road parking space and looked over at Peace Cottage. The place had definite kerb appeal. It sat well in the rural surroundings but wasn't too prettily twee. Solidly constructed from bricks and slate, no thatched roof or whitewash to cause maintenance problems. It was old enough to have interesting period features and a bit of history, but also benefitted from central heating and a new bathroom. He walked down the path in the neat front garden and let himself in. Immediately a feeling of contentment seemed to wrap itself around him.

He walked through the light, spacious rooms, stopping to look out at the view of hills in the distance. The garden at the moment was easy maintenance but it was big enough to take a vegetable patch if anyone wanted one, or even a greenhouse. Yes, plenty of potential there. In his head he was composing the blurb to go out to prospective customers, but for once he didn't have to exaggerate, bend the truth or tactfully leave out a few details. This place was perfect. He'd have no trouble selling it.

Avril followed the estate agent's car to Peace Cottage. If it even halfway lived up to its name she was going to buy it. She passed a school so close her two could walk there. How wonderful not to have to battle traffic for the school run every day.

As she stepped inside, Avril felt a sense of calm. Yes, this was just what she needed. There was an en suite bathroom for the main bedroom. She allowed herself to imagine the luxury of ten minutes alone in there without someone banging on the door saying they needed the loo, or had a crisis she must sort out. From the window she saw a swing and a garden plenty big enough for children to play.

The main bedroom wasn't large, but had room for a double bed which was more than she'd need without Duke to share it. King-size would seem too big, too lonely. Two box rooms would be adequate for her children. No room for drum kits; bliss!

No room for her step-children to stay over though. Her children, his children; she hadn't thought of them that way in years. They didn't themselves, they were brothers and sisters to each other. A unit. They were her family. Yes, they squabbled, it was noisy and chaotic and she never had a moment to herself, but she loved them. She couldn't just walk out when all she really needed was a few moments to herself now and then. She'd go home and explain that to Duke. They'd sort something out. Maybe she'd take up yoga. Duke could rush round getting everyone to Brownies and Scouts and the swimming baths, dropping her off at the community centre. Or she could walk there.

"It's lovely, but sorry it's not for me," Avril said.

Richard sighed. He'd got his hopes up when she'd first seen it and imagined a quick sale. That would have got his partner off his back and stopped him saying Richard was getting too old for this game. How he'd have liked to make a simple, honest straightforward sale without all the ludicrously low offers, time wasters without mortgages, gazumping and broken chains.

Thomas said he'd like to make his own way to Peace Cottage and get a feel for the area first. He enjoyed lunch in the pub which, if he took the footpath, would be within easy walking distance. The friendly landlord pulled a decent pint and when Thomas explained why he was there a couple of locals told him it was a nice place, they thought he'd like it. Reassuringly there didn't seem to be a sign of resenting the newcomer.

He arrived early so had a look round the outside. Everything had been maintained very well. The gutters looked to be efficient, the fence was in good repair, the windows were those modern sealed units which never needed anything doing to them. The garden too was well done. Evergreen shrubs would give year round colour and structure. The grass had proper edging, so would just need a quick going over with a mower to keep it in order.

Richard arrived and introduced himself, then his phone rang. "Sorry, there's been a bit of a crisis, I'd better..."

Thomas indicated for him to go ahead. As a businessman himself he knew how important it could be to act quickly. After a moment or two of trying not to listen but realising the issue was complicated, he mimed unlocking the door. Richard looked relieved as he handed over the key for Thomas to look round by himself.

Inside the cottage, Thomas relaxed. He didn't need Richard to point out the neat, fully fitted kitchen, the sanded floor-boards, the nicely decorated rooms. It was perfect. He couldn't fault anything, wouldn't want to change anything and neither would Laura... so what would he do with himself? True he'd decided he'd had enough of the stresses and strains of running his own construction company and

81

wanted to slow down, but not to stop entirely. This place was too peaceful, too quiet. It would be for Laura too. She always enjoyed picking out colour schemes for the houses he'd built, the homes he'd renovated. She had a real eye for it and knew just which curtains would billow in the breeze to give a feeling of space, could spot exactly the right carpet to transform a poky space into a snug and cosy room. She'd want to do that for their home too. She probably wasn't quite ready to sit looking at him day in day out either. No, he'd be better off buying somewhere which needed work, which they could shape and make their own and which would keep him occupied as he adjusted to a quieter pace of life.

"It's a nice place," Thomas said when Richard eventually joined him. "New instruction isn't it?"

"Yes it is and I'd advise you to make an offer quickly if you're interested. Lots of other people are." Usually he'd hint something like that, but in this case it was perfectly true.

"Don't suppose the owners will accept an offer then?"

"No. I imagine it will get close to the asking price, possibly even a bit more."

"Not like that place you're offering in Kent Road. Been on the market long has it?"

"Er, a little while, yes."

"They might take an offer there?"

"I think they'd consider it." They'd snap his hand off. The place was a tip and needed a lot doing to it, plus they'd taken no notice of Richard's advice to declutter and redecorate in a less flamboyant style.

Thomas seemed delighted at the prospect of all that work, all that stress, which was good if it meant he could sell the awful place on Kent Road, but Richard couldn't understand why anyone could prefer it to Peace Cottage. After listening on the phone to one prospective customer in floods of tears because the survey on the property she was offering had revealed problems of which she'd been unaware, the anger of the people above and below her in the chain and the exasperation of his partner, Richard was wishing his retirement date was closer, not hoping to push it back.

Richard stepped into Peace Cottage just to check all the lights were off. That sense of tranquility washed over him again. Thomas would buy the place on Kent Road, he'd see beyond the superficial to the potential. Peace Cottage was so perfect it would find a buyer very soon. It was all going to be OK.

Phoebe thought the cottage was kind of sweet, but boy was it out in the sticks. Would any of her friends visit? She doubted it. She could just hear them now, telling her not to waste her time sitting around waiting for Lawrence and come spend the weekend with them instead.

"Quite convenient for the train," Richard said.

The garden was pretty, she liked flowers and maybe she could get in a gardener. A fit, strong young man to clip the hedges and dig, shirtless in the ground.

Inside the cottage she felt her spirits lift. It was an ideal love nest for when Lawrence could get away. Very discreet. They wouldn't see anyone they knew. It was near his elderly parents so he could pop in to see them and tell his wife he was staying over...

Phoebe opened a cupboard, saw a skeleton and screamed.

"It's just a mouse," Richard said. "The previous owner had

a cat and it must have left this."

Oh great! A skeleton in the cupboard. Just a tiny one and easily dealt with. Unlike her. She was Lawrence's metaphoric skeleton in the cupboard, wasn't she? Other men she'd dated had been proud to show her off, introduce her to their friends and family, but not Lawrence. At first it had seemed exciting to be the secret lover of an older man, someone important and well respected. But he didn't really deserve all that respect did he? The good family man had a secret: her.

What was she thinking wasting her time with him? His wife probably thought he was faithful and loved her but he wasn't. He didn't really love Phoebe either, did he? She'd tell him it was over, get back her self-respect and her life!

Phoebe kissed Richard and was gone.

How odd. Everyone he showed the cottage to said it was wonderful, perfect. When they stepped inside it seemed like their worries and cares were soothed away and they all left full of hope and enthusiasm, but they never put in an offer.

What was wrong with them all? The place in Kent Road which was hideous had sold. The flat where the three previous occupants had in turn all died under odd circumstances had sold. The place which flooded every other year, the houses next to a slaughterhouse, with rising damp, dry rot and neighbours from hell had all sold. They'd been a struggle, causing him to lose more of his grey hairs and added to the lines on his face, but they'd sold. Why not Peace Cottage?

He understood different people had different needs and nowhere was perfect for everyone. He understood too that feeling people sometimes got of a place just not being right for them. That never happened at Peace Cottage; everyone liked it. They said so. Richard was used to seeing beyond the words to what they really meant. They did mean it when they said they liked Peace Cottage and when they said they wouldn't buy it. Here there was never an insincere, 'we'll think it over' or 'we'll be in touch' but always a definite no.

He couldn't understand it. Maybe there was something he'd missed?

Richard let himself in and was instantly reassured. This place was perfect.

His phone rang. It was his partner demanding to know if he'd made the sale.

"I have two offers for you."

"Oh great, a bidding war!" He sounded happy for once.

"No. Just one offer for the cottage, but for the full asking price"

"OK, good."

"But it's subject to another sale."

"Isn't it always? Is that one of ours?"

"It is, but it could just be yours, if you'll buy me out."

There was silence on the other end of the phone, but Richard knew the other man was thinking it over. He closed his phone, stepped into Peace Cottage and knew that after dealing with thousands of flats, houses and apartments, he'd at last found a home.

14 Camellia

Alex studied his reflection in the mirror; pretty good. His suit was perfect, his shave close, shoes and hair both gleaming. He tugged gently on his sleeves to ensure they were exactly level. His mum had sometimes teased him for preening.

"Like a bird, Mum? No, I'm more of a cat person. Elegant and graceful."

"Yes with your fussy ways I suppose you are." She always laughed though when she said anything like that. How he missed her.

Alex would have made a good cat he was sure. He was fastidious, attractive and self-contained. A Siamese perhaps, or a sleek black one with spotless white feet, bib and tail tip. That's just how he felt now in his suit; like a cat ready to pounce on his prize.

The meeting would go well, he just knew. At least he was fairly sure. His new job meant he'd have more stability, more to offer. Alex hoped it was be enough for Chrissie. Once again he wondered if he'd done the right thing in proposing. She'd asked for time to think and would give him an answer today. If she said 'no' where would that leave their relationship?

He looked at his reflection again and ruffled his hair so it wasn't completely perfect. Alex pulled at his tie so the knot was askew. No; too obvious. He adjusted it again. He was what he was, no point pretending otherwise.

As he turned from locking his front door, Alex caught sight of his neighbour. He called out a greeting but she didn't react. Odd. Mrs Roberts seized every chance she got for a chat. He didn't mind, she'd been lovely to him when he'd first moved in after his mum's death.

"Mrs Roberts?" he called more loudly.

There was still no reply. Her shoulders were hunched and she was shaking so he jumped over the fence. When he got close he saw he'd guessed correctly and she was crying.

"Are you OK?" It was a stupid question but perhaps better than none.

She held out a camellia bloom. "I just picked this to take indoors. Isn't it perfect?"

"It is, yes." He'd noticed the shrub with its opulent blooms so flawless they hardly seemed real and intended to ask if he might pick a few the next time he entertained. Their refined simplicity would be the ideal table decoration.

Alex smiled encouragingly at his neighbour. If she wanted to talk about whatever had upset her he could spare a minute to listen.

"They never used to be perfect. The plant was here before I moved in with Tiddles. When it flowered every blossom was ragged. Very strange looking. More like tassels than petals they were."

"How peculiar."

"That's what I thought. The bush was quite big by then and I couldn't imagine why it had been kept unless it was a rare type or something. I asked about and was told the flowers always used to be perfect. In fact the previous owner had won prizes with them at the local show."

"They're perfect again now. I wonder if you'll ever solve the mystery of what happened to them?"

"I did." She blew her nose. "It was Tiddles. He used to shred them. Can't think why, but it didn't do him any harm as he lived twenty-three years which is incredibly long for a cat. As the bush got bigger, and he got less agile, more and more blossoms were spared. Last year they were all perfect."

"When he was ill?" She'd had a poorly cat when he moved in almost a year ago. It died soon after and Alex had never seen him.

"Yes. I actually picked him a few to play with."

"Did he?"

"Yes, then slept and never woke up. I really miss him..."

"I'm so sorry." Alex placed a hand on her shoulder.

After a moment she seemed to make an effort to pull herself together. "Sorry to make a fuss and bless you for coming over to look after me. I thought the gate was locked though, I must be getting forgetful."

"Actually I jumped the fence."

"Gracious. You're like a cat yourself!"

"Ah, that's why you like me! I take it as a compliment. Cats are so elegant and kind of aloof. I'd like to give that impression but I'd never pull it off."

"No. You're not uncaring like a lot of youths. I read about the horrible things teenagers do and then think of you to restore my faith in human nature."

Alex liked to think he was an OK bloke, but that was going a bit far.

"I was reading in the newspaper this morning about a poor cat that had been tormented by some boys after it was abandoned."

No wonder she was upset.

"I'd like to rescue him myself, but I'm too old to take on a new pet. It's just a kitten. If it lives to the same age as Tiddles I'd be 106 by the time he died."

"I wouldn't put it past you to live that long, especially with an animal to look after, but I do see your point. Look... I'd love a cat myself but as you know I'm away a lot with work. That's just about to change though and I'll be home much more. What about we see if we can rescue that poor little creature together?"

Her whole face smiled. "Really? You'd do that? And if something happens to me..."

"If either of us can't care for him for any reason, the other will take over, yes."

"Shall we ring the rescue place now? The number is in the newspaper."

"OK then."

"Come in with me and I'll make you a cup of coffee."

"Sorry, Mrs Roberts I can't stay. I was on my way to an important meeting when I saw you were upset..."

"I've held you up. I'm so sorry."

"It'll be OK. I'm sure Chrissie will understand but I must go."

"Yes, of course. When will you be back? I'll come round

and we can talk about the cat."

"You ring up and arrange for us to go this afternoon or tomorrow and I'll drive us in, OK?"

"I will and say hello to that lovely young lady of yours. I hope you'll think about marrying her."

"OK, I will. Now I really must go."

Alex leapt back over the fence, snagging his trousers as he did. There was no time to change his clothes, a thing he was quite incapable of doing quickly, so he got in the car just as he was and drove to the coffee shop. It was a good sign Chrissie had suggested meeting there, wasn't it? It's where they'd gone on their first date. He was sure she wouldn't have forgotten that. He arrived only slightly late but red-faced and more than a little dishevelled.

Chrissie was waiting outside. "Alex, what's happened?" she asked before he reached her. "Is something wrong?"

"No, no. Not at all." He hugged her. "My neighbour, Mrs Roberts you know?"

Chrissie nodded.

"She was upset so I was talking to her and..." Oh gosh he'd agreed to share a cat with her. He shouldn't have done that without thinking it through. He never did anything without thinking it through and this was an important decision. One Chrissie should have been involved in. At least if she gave him the answer he'd been hoping for she should be consulted. In a way he'd not done it without thinking. He'd wanted a cat for some time now, had always wanted one if her were honest.

"Well? What's happened to Mrs Roberts?"

He explained the whole story, then turned to show her the hole in his trousers. She laughed which he thought was a good sign. Maybe she wouldn't agree to marry him but she wasn't the kind of girl to laugh at a man just before she dumped him.

"I should have waited until I got your answer, I'm sorry about that."

"I'm not, Alex."

"No?"

"Let's go in and get a coffee and then we can talk."

Waiting for the drinks to be made gave Alex an unwelcome opportunity to think. Did she mean she was glad he was getting a cat because it was the only creature he'd be sharing his life with?

They carried their coffees to a table tucked away in the corner.

Chrissie leant across and took his hand. "I was going to say no, Alex. I do love you and want to keep seeing you, that's why I asked you to meet me here... to show it didn't have to be over."

"Going to say no?"

"Yes. You're so perfect. Always looking wonderful."

"So do you!"

"Thanks but I wasn't fishing for compliments. You're always spotless. My hair's always falling out of its clips and I've usually got paint under my fingernails and sometimes I'm wearing odd shoes."

"Yes, but what does that matter?"

"And your house gleams. Everything is in its place. There

are no paint brushes left on chairs. You never burn dinner because you were so engrossed in what you were doing..."

He clearly hadn't properly communicated his vision of the future to her. His attic, with a little work and the addition of several skylights, would make the perfect studio for her. All her work clutter could stay up there without causing him any concern and he'd carry on doing the cleaning and cooking. His lovely, talented, chaotic Chrissie wasn't cut out for that kind of work.

He tried to explain but she cut him off. "It's all right, Alex. You did say all that before."

"But you're still going to say no?"

"No. I still was going to say no. I know you think you can confine my mess to one room, but I'll still leave clothes on the bedroom floor and my coffee cup wherever I happen to be once I've finished my drink. I'll forget I have paint on my hands and leave little smears everywhere."

"I'll forgive you."

"I know you will, just like you forgive Mrs Roberts for making you late by keeping you talking. I know now that you can cope with imperfection too. You must have wanted to change your ripped trousers?"

"Off course, but then I'd have kept you waiting."

"And I'm more important to you than how perfect you look?"

"Of course!"

"I believe you now, but I wasn't quite sure before. Now, this cat you're getting, tell me about it."

"I doubt we'll get the one mentioned in the paper. A cute

little kitten that's had this kind of publicity should easily find a home, but I'm confident we can provide a good home for a cat that needs it."

"They all shed hair all the time you know."

"I know. I expect I'll be spending more time vacuuming."

"I expect so."

As Alex had predicted they didn't get the kitten Mrs Roberts had seen in the paper. They didn't get any cat right away, but eventually Alex and Mrs Roberts adopted a cat between them. They called her Camellia. The name was the only elegant thing about her. She too had been badly treated in the past. Poor mite had patches where hair was missing. The end of her tail had been broken and was permanently kinked. She was scrawny too. They soon got her back to a healthy weight but she retained the bald patches. That didn't stop her shedding hair everywhere though. Alex vacuumed more frequently than previously but it was a small price to pay for the pleasure Camellia brought him and Mrs Roberts.

A year later, Alex studied his reflection in the mirror: pretty good. His suit was perfect, his shave close, shoes and hair both gleaming. He tugged gently on his sleeves to ensure they were exactly level.

"Lovely!" Mrs Roberts exclaimed as she dabbed at him with sticky tape to remove the worst of the cat hairs. "Are you ready?"

Alex tucked a perfect Camellia bud into his buttonhole, knowing it would match Chrissie's bridal bouquet. "I'm ready."

15 Breaking With Routine

Long before tea break, colleagues surrounded my desk. Everyone held something; a card, flowers, cake.

"Well, this is a surprise!" It wasn't. They've been discussing my retirement for weeks. I'd enjoyed my job, but it was time to go and I was looking forward to the change, despite what people seemed to think.

I gave up all attempts to work as an array of baked goodies were spread across my desk. Cakes are something of a tradition in the office. Birthdays, payday. The boss once bought everyone a doughnut on a miserable Monday because our office chairs were three years old. She's a lovely lady, Jean, very caring. She asked if there was anything she could do to help me adapt to retirement. I assured her I was fully prepared.

Jean formally thanked me for my years of service and meticulous time-keeping. There were grins and nodded heads at that. I smiled back. I know my careful punctuality really is appreciated even if some of the younger ones find it amusing.

Jean handed me flowers, a prettily wrapped package and card. "A little something for you to remember us by, Primrose."

"Thank you."

"Speech, speech," called someone.

"All in good time," I said. That got a laugh.

The card was gorgeous. Hand-made with pressed flowers, including primroses, naturally. Everyone had written in it. There were poems; some moving, some a little cheeky. There were remembrances of pleasant or amusing incidents from my working life and thanks from staff I'd trained. I read them all out, playing for time.

"There's these too." I was given three tiny canvas bags each containing a potted primrose. "I expect you already have lots, but these were so sweet we couldn't resist."

"You can never have too much of a good thing," I assured them before opening the wrapped gift. Thankfully it wasn't the right shape or weight to be a clock. Although I'd treasure it as a memento I already had sufficient, perfectly accurate, clocks.

Inside primrose printed paper was the most lovely notebook. It matched the card with its cover of pressed flowers. The pages were as velvety as petals. It would be such a pleasure to use. There was a pen too, a proper fountain pen in primrose yellow.

"These are just lovely. Thank you so much."

They seemed to be waiting for something. After a moment I spotted it, a plain envelope containing garden centre vouchers, a ridiculously generous quantity of them.

Giving in to their demands for a speech I said that although I'd miss my job, and them, I was looking forward to retirement and to writing the book on the history of primroses I'd been researching for years. I kept my attention on the time. Stopping at eleven I declared it was exactly time for our tea break. That got another little laugh before we started on the cakes.

Later I overheard myself being discussed. Someone said how nice it was I had an interest to occupy me in retirement.

"It is, because heaven knows what she'll do without the routine of the office," a friend replied.

"Don't worry about me, girls," I said. "I'm looking forward to a complete break from routine."

They didn't look convinced.

I remembered that every morning the following week as, even without setting the alarm, I awoke at my usual time. There was no need to get up; I was free from the need to stick to my careful routine. Freedom is choice though and I decided I didn't have to stay in bed either.

OK I admit it. It's three months now and I still get up at the same time as I always have. Instead of driving to work I walk around my garden. I reach my desk and begin work at nine exactly. I stop at one for lunch and return to my desk until five. I still do my main grocery shopping on Saturday and still buy special cakes on the last Thursday of the month.

Why not? I'm happy. And don't go thinking I'm stuck in a rut. Some days I work away from home, in the library, gardens or at nurseries which stock primroses. I always take my lovely new pen and notebook with me, to record anything I learn. Even at home I vary my routine. Yesterday I had my morning tea break at ten fifteen and this afternoon I've taken two, both of which I enjoyed in the garden and I've stayed out here, barefoot and wearing nothing but a bikini top and shorts as I work. I doubt they'll be introducing that in your office any time soon.

16 Emily's Error

Emily should have known looking at the handsome stranger's patient file would lead to trouble, but she hadn't stopped to think. Almost every day for weeks she'd seen him at Fleur's coffee shop. Often they almost bumped into each other when one left as the other arrived. He always smiled at her, sometimes adding a comment about the weather. Emily always smiled back, but never spoke.

Then last week, as she'd left the coffee shop, he'd walked past, rather than going in. He smiled and said, 'hello' before falling into step beside her.

"I hope you haven't given up coffee?" she blurted out, then blushed as she realised she'd made it clear she looked forward to seeing him.

"Not at all. I'll be in at the usual time tomorrow. See you then?"

Emily nodded. Was he hinting he didn't mind being seen?

When they reached the dental surgery she stopped. "This is where I work."

He opened the door for her – and followed her in! She raced to the safety of the rest room to gulp her coffee.

Emily returned to reception and fiddled out with the vase of carnations on the counter.

"Anya, did that man register as a patient?" she asked, as casually as she could.

"Yes. Poor chap seemed rather surprised to be in a dental surgery, but once he got over the shock he signed up. Hey, he's not your man from the coffee shop is he?"

"Yes." Of course he'd never really be her man, but that wasn't what Anya meant.

"That explains it. He must have followed you here and when you disappeared out the back he was stuck with me."

Emily would have disagreed with that, but knew Anya would just tell her to have more confidence.

Anya tapped her in tray invitingly. "I have his file here."

Emily had no good reason for taking a look, but couldn't help herself. She wanted to know his name and check when his appointment was scheduled to make sure she was working that day. The idea of him in the chair and it being her job to look at, and look after him was very appealing. Trouble was, she also saw his address. It wasn't that far out of her way as she walked into work and Valentine's Day was tomorrow – too late for the post.

She bought a card and addressed it simply 'Mark'. Hopefully the lobby of the flats where he lived would be open in the morning to allow the postman in. It seemed she was in luck, right up until she took the card from her bag and stepped over to the bank of tin boxes. The lift pinged, the doors slid open and Mark stepped out. Why hadn't it occurred to her he was likely to be leaving for work about now? Emily dropped her hand and shoved the card into the box below his. Then she ran.

"What on earth's the matter?" Anya asked as Emily arrived, red and flustered at work.

Emily confessed, much to Anya's amusement.

"It's not funny, Anya! Now he'll think I'm interested in one of his neighbours."

"Well, you can explain when you see him in the coffee shop."

"No, I couldn't. Really, I couldn't."

"You should explain. And what about the poor man who gets your card? What's his wife going to think?"

Emily felt sick. Why oh why, had she ever looked at Mark's file? She didn't have the confidence to explain to him about the card. She completely avoided the coffee shop.

Worry about the trouble she might have caused the recipient of her card played on her mind all morning. By lunchtime she felt so guilty she returned to the block of flats. By squinting through the now secured door, she read the number on the box into which she'd shoved the card. Emily took a deep breath and rang the bell.

"Hello?" a tinny, female sounding voice came from the speaker.

"Hello, I er, made a mistake this morning. Er, that is I... "

"I think you'd better come up."

With a pounding heart, Emily entered the building, travelled up in the lift and looked down the corridor.

A door swung open and an elderly lady looked out. "Was it you who sent the card?"

Emily nodded.

The lady beamed. "Come in then, dear."

Relieved she wasn't annoyed, Emily did as she was asked and accepted the offer of a cup of tea. The lady was easy to talk to and sympathetic as Emily explained what happened.

"Don't worry, dear. There's no harm done." She returned the unopened envelope to Emily.

A buzzer sounded.

"Excuse me." The lady went to her door.

Emily heard a man's voice say, "Sorry to bother you, but I think someone accidentally left a card for me in your mail box."

"Are you Mark?" the lady asked.

"Yes."

"Come in then."

Emily felt her heart pound again.

The lady returned to her lounge, followed by Mark who was carrying a bouquet of pale pink gerberas, tiny daisies and spray carnations.

"I took these to the coffee shop, but must have missed you so I went to the surgery in my lunch break. Your colleague told me why you were here this morning and that you'd come back."

Emily couldn't speak, but she did pass him the card as she accepted her flowers.

17 Family Business

Looking back, I never thought I could really be Mum's child. She was so perfect, always. Never a hair out of place or chipped nail. She looked like what she was; the owner of a classy dress shop. I was a tomboy who didn't care what I looked like.

"This blue velvet will bring out the colour of your eyes, Chloe," she would say as she buttoned me into a dress. The colour was all right, much better than the pinks and other bright shades she favoured to show off her much darker eyes and complexion, but I'd have preferred it to be made into dungarees. Or she'd say, "This skirt will go well with your uniform sweatshirt." Trousers would have done the job just as well, I thought.

Mum didn't like the baggy sweatshirt. "My school uniform was a gingham dress and blazer. You'd have looked so smart in that."

She was probably glad though that the practical top with its dark colour didn't show grass stains. I liked it because it was warm and looked the same whatever I'd done, so saved me from many a, "I can't think what you've been doing," after a lunch break game of football.

My idea of wearing the right clothes was to put on wellies when it rained and chose trousers thick enough not to rip when I climbed trees. Mum would have loved me to wear the kind of thing her shop supplied to more ladylike girls and their mothers.

We didn't row about clothes because we didn't row about anything. Neither of us wanted to hurt the other, but it niggled that I was almost never out of her sight and that she wanted me to be neat and pretty. I hated to be fussed over or restrained in any way. She'd make me pretty little dresses that I usually managed to drip mud on before she'd finished stitching up the hem. The ringlets she coaxed into my hair didn't disguise the bruises and scratches I was generally covered in. I could no more sit still than she could have run down the street making Indian war cries with the boys next door. That we were so different must have been as much of a trial to her as it was to me, but I never doubted she loved me very much.

I had a bit more in common with Dad, though I looked even less like him than I did Mum. I liked being down the allotment with him, watching things grow and harvesting them. It wasn't a regular allotment with other people all round, but a piece of waste ground behind his office that he worked in when everyone else went home. I liked the peace and quiet there, that no one bothered us, and how riotously abundant it looked in the summer. It seemed a shame though that no one took much notice of the results. No one except us and Mum. She cooked the fruit and vegetables into tidy meals that I wolfed down before running out to play again.

Often I came home with bags bursting with potatoes or baskets overflowing with strawberries (although I reduced that overflow considerably by eating it on the walk home). What I liked best was picking great bunches of dahlias and arriving home with my arms tiring under the weight of the gaudy blooms.

"Look, Mum, aren't they pretty?" I asked shaking out the last of the earwigs the first year Dad grew them.

Suppressing a shudder Mum said, "They are, Chloe. Perhaps you'd like to help me arrange them?"

That was our one mother and daughter thing. I picked flowers for her, filled vases with water and Mum made neat arrangements for our home and her shop. I didn't have the patience to fiddle about so every stem was at exactly the right angle and trimmed to the perfect height, but I was good at selecting the best blooms to bring home and choosing which foliage would set them off.

When I was about ten, Dad asked his boss if I could take over a patch of ground next to his to grow more flowers.

"Do anything you like out there as long as you keep it tidy," the older man told us.

Dad grinned. "Just like being at home eh? Keep things tidy and everyone's happy."

He had a point about the tidiness, and about doing as I wanted. If my parents had been even slightly more lenient or generous then I'd definitely have been classified as spoiled. I was an only child and Mum and Dad were a fair bit older than me. They, especially Mum, often referred to me as 'our little miracle'. If I wanted to go somewhere, they took me. If I wanted something I was often bought it and I never lacked for attention. Other kids used to yell, 'watch me' if they wanted a witness to their daring on the slide in the playground, or brilliance at skipping. I never needed to ask.

My life continued carefree except for the occasional insistence that I allow Mum to 'do something about that hair' or put on pretty clothes and sit quietly for a while so her friends could admire me. Sometimes I was asked to model clothes she'd made. I didn't mind doing that too much as it was to help her, not just to make me look girly and nice.

When I went to secondary school, with its proper uniform, Mum insisted on tailoring my clothes from good quality material. She made more trousers than skirts though and ensured every item was loose enough that I could run and jump without fear of rips. I probably had a few pre-teen strops, but I don't remember there being any real unease.

Then at school we did a project about the changes which had happened in our lifetime. It was really weird to know that our present would become other people's history. People brought in photos of themselves taken at places which had since been closed down, or turned into something else. Mine showed me and Mum outside her shop the day she moved to her current premises. We all brought in our birth certificates. Some were much bigger than my little square of paper. They showed their parents' names, as well as their own and said where the birth had taken place.

"The shorter ones are copies," our teacher explained. "That's not at all unusual as people often lose the original."

Maybe so, but not my mum. She didn't lose things. She kept all her paperwork neatly organised in folders. She had stuff for the shop, drawings I'd done at play group, their original marriage certificate and things dating back to her own school days. I knew because I'd seen them. There were things I'd never seen though. Pictures of Mum looking pregnant for example. I'd never asked why I didn't have her and Dad's dark hair, but I did ask about the lack of photos.

"Maternity wear is rarely glamorous, Chloe," she said.

I knew something was bothering her though because she picked up her hand cream and applied it without first taking off her rings.

The school project involved looking at newspaper headlines for the week we were born. I discovered a baby had been snatched from outside a dress shop when I was just a few days old. Once I saw it, every headline seemed to blur into one about babies and dress shops. Well, just one dress shop; Mum's old place. She'd moved from there when I was a toddler. Was it to avoid being associated with that stolen child?

I didn't ask my parents about it. I wanted them to reassure me, but wasn't sure they could. Instead I looked up the address of the woman whose baby was snatched. That wasn't difficult and didn't arouse concern, as naturally my classmates were of a similar age and also interested in the story. She'd lived in a part of town I'd not really visited. Mum once said it was a rough area. Maybe she had another reason for not wanting me to go there?

My bus pass didn't cover me for that route and it seemed wrong to use the pocket money my parents had given me, so I sent a text to say I'd be late home from school and walked. Part of the journey took me past two men swearing at each other in the street, and some boarded-over shop fronts. Perhaps twenty minutes later I reached my destination.

The house was about the same size as ours but the garden was much bigger. There was a sign outside saying 'eggs and flowers for sale'. Under it was a table holding boxes of eggs and a tin labelled 'honesty box'. Under the table, in the shade, were buckets full of flowers. Curious, I looked inside the tin and saw quite a bit of money.

I walked down the path, which was really just a track through the grass. On one side was a big tree with a tyre swing. On the other was an abandoned game of cricket. When I reached the porch I saw dirty wellies chucked in a heap. I knocked loudly and shouted, but nobody came to gasp at the sight of blue eyes which mirrored theirs, or to offer big wedges of cake baked with their own eggs, or even invite me to play cricket. Somehow I'd imagined all that happening as I'd walked from gate to door. I scribbled a note saying I thought I might be their daughter, added my mobile number and left.

When I got back to just before where the men had been arguing I started to get a bit nervous. I wasn't used to being on my own in a strange place. Other than school, or visits to friends for tea I was always with one or other of my parents. If they weren't there, one of them had walked me to the bus stop or driven me to where I was going and hadn't left until I was in the company of people I knew.

It was quite a relief when Mum rang, anxious to know if I was OK and where I was. My voice wobbled as I read the street name off the graffiti covered sign. Mum and Dad arrived so quickly she couldn't have driven as neatly and carefully as usual. She leapt out and hugged me without stopping to close the door. Dad squeezed my shoulder, then drove us home. My explanation probably didn't make much sense, but clearly Mum got the gist of it as when we got in she made me hot chocolate and told me I was adopted.

"I know we should have told you before, but when you were just about old enough to understand we took you to a carnival. You wriggled through the crowd to get a better look and got lost. You were so scared by the time we found you, thinking you'd never see us again. We wanted to wait until you were over that before telling you and the longer we left it the harder it got."

Mum fetched one of her tidy files and showed me more press clippings from around the time of my birth. I'd seen some of the reports before at school, but after that first one I'd not taken in any details. My parents sat either side of me as I read. A baby had indeed been snatched from a pram outside the shop. She wasn't me and had soon been returned to her parents.

"The poor woman who took her had suffered a late miscarriage. I could understand the longing for a child. Your Dad and I were going through the adoption process at the time."

What had I been thinking? Of course my parents hadn't just stolen me from outside Mum's shop and carried on living with me in the same town. They wouldn't do such an awful thing and couldn't have got away with it if they did.

Mum put her hand on my arm. "Then you were abandoned on the doorstep. That I couldn't understand. I knew there are cases where women were forced by circumstances to give up their children as that's what we were waiting for. But you were a month old, clean and well fed. You were dressed in a sweet little outfit and wrapped in a blanket. Very fine cashmere, new and expensive so it didn't seem she couldn't afford to feed you or was unable to cope."

"Maybe she wanted you to adopt me?"

"Perhaps so. It was suggested she'd read the reports in the

paper about the abduction and that the owner of the shop wanted a child. But I'm not so sure. There was no note and you were left for hours before I came to open up. I had to get you straight to hospital. There were better ways she could have gone about it."

She didn't raise her voice but I'd never heard her sound so angry. Dad spoke softly to her, but I was no longer listening. I was thinking of the note I'd left for that other mother. What pain might I have reminded her of?

Mum touched my unhappy face. "I'm sorry... We said we'd never speak against her and I wanted to spare you all that. That's partly why we didn't tell you before. I couldn't think of a way to explain you were adopted without telling you how you were left."

I nodded to show I understood. I wasn't angry, perhaps because it wasn't really a big shock that I wasn't their biological child.

"They traced her then?" I asked.

"Yes. Your case worker said they had and she quickly signed the paperwork for your adoption, that's something at least. We didn't meet her or anything, probably it wouldn't have been allowed but we didn't try. Her details might be on your records though. We can ask if you like."

Before I could even wonder if I was ready to know more, my phone beeped indicating a text. Without thinking, I pulled it from my pocket and read, 'Got your message. Please call me'.

I briefly explained to my parents about the note I'd left earlier that day, then called the woman to apologise. I didn't get far before she said, "Chloe, calm down. You haven't upset me. Actually I think I might be about to upset you. I'm sorry, but I'm not your mother."

By then I knew she couldn't be. I'd been so sure when I was stood on the doorstep. Sure I'd found my biological mother and sure that's what I wanted. My logic had been all mixed up. There were two babies, one which had been snatched then returned to the mother who very much wanted it and me who'd been abandoned by a mother who didn't want her at all.

"I think you're confusing me with the person who lived here before. That was a few years ago and I don't have an address, but maybe the council have records?"

I thanked her, apologised again and disconnected. Thank goodness I'd not hurt her. Not wanting to hurt people was something I'd got from Mum. My real one, the one who'd brought me up, not the one who left me outside a shop. It seemed to me Mum was right about her not reading the local papers. I had to hope she was upset about leaving me and struggling to cope so wouldn't have had time to read about other people's troubles. She'd wrapped me warmly and left me where I'd be found by the person who's been my mum ever since. It could have been worse.

"I'm so sorry, Chloe," Mum said. "We should have told you long ago."

We talked for a while longer. My parents explaining the processes they'd had to go through to make me theirs. They excused me from school for what was the last two days before half-term. They contacted social services and a lady explained to me how I could try to contact my birth mother. I've kept the information as I might want to do that sometime, but not yet. I was all talked out by the time I got back to school. Of course I told my friends I was adopted. Other than concern I might be upset it didn't matter to them at all. I can't say it mattered to me much either by then. I handed my project in slightly late as it was due while I was off school, but I got an A. Mum and Dad were proud and rightly so as it shows what a great job they'd done bringing me up.

Things haven't changed a lot since then. Mum still wants to pretty me up and I'm still digging in my patch of ground with Dad. That's coming on really well. I don't just grow dahlias, but have different flowers pretty much all year round. They start with early daffodils and tulips, go through wallflowers, sweet peas, cosmos, marigolds and larkspur until the first dahlias bloom. They're still my favourites, but zinnias and chrysanthemums are great too.

I give some of each kind to Mum for her tidy arrangements and more than double my pocket money by selling the rest as loose posies to the people who work in Dad's office. I offered a discount to his boss as it was his ground they grew in. He became my best customer, regularly buying flowers for his desk and to take home for his wife.

One evening I heard Dad tell Mum what his boss had said about me. "'Proper little entrepreneur your daughter, just like that lovely wife of yours with her business. I hope you're not going to follow their example and leave me to set up on your own?' I didn't know quite what to say."

"I do," I said, making them jump. I suppose they hadn't realised I could hear them. "It's the gardening I get from you, Dad. The business stuff all comes from Mum."

I said the bit about gardening just to please him. Really we're not a bit alike, me with my gorgeous flowers and him with his boring old cabbages and leeks. No, I'm much more like Mum. She started dress-making at school, earning a few pennies by taking up hems and letting out seams and built up her business from there.

One day I'll have my own florist shop and every day, just like Mum, I'll be surrounded by colour, texture and prettiness. I'm her daughter through and through.

18 Payback Time

"The lad on holiday, is he?" Malcolm, the warden, asked.

We looked at the weeds on Ian's normally immaculate allotment.

I shrugged. "He didn't say anything."

"Not like him to let weeds grow and there's beans need picking... Think he's OK?"

"He's a good strong chap."

"Unless he did his back in, doing all that digging for you. Not trying to get extra business for your old medical practice, are you?"

I must have looked worried, because Malcolm said, "Don't worry, Bert; I was just teasing. He'll be on holiday again, I expect."

I nodded, but I wasn't so sure. Young Ian did go away a fair bit, but he always said and asked me to water for him. He always asked what I wanted brought back. I asked for a pyramid when he went to Egypt. He gave me a brick as the first instalment. I got a box of sand when I'd asked for a Caribbean beach. He presented me with a bottle of water, when he returned from a swanky hotel, saying it was an ice sculpture.

I never wanted a real gift; Ian did so much of the digging and mowing on my plot that he'd amply repaid anything I did for him. Tell the truth, I'd probably have given up my plot if it wasn't for Ian.

Try as I might, I couldn't remember if he'd been down the allotments since he'd finished my digging. I hadn't seen him, but that wasn't surprising. I tend to do my gardening in the mornings and he does his after work. It was only on weekends we met. He hadn't been there last weekend.

I left a note on his shed door and decided if it was still there in the morning I'd go and see if he was OK. He'd told me which road he lived in and I knew what his car looked like, so I reckoned I could find the right house.

My note and Ian's weeds were still there the next morning. I didn't even unlock my own shed but went straight round to Ian's home. His car was on the driveway so I knocked on the door. After a couple of minutes an upstairs window opened and Ian called out, "Hello?"

I stepped back a bit so he could see me. "Are you all right?"

"Not really, I've done my back in."

Oh dear, it was just as I'd feared. "Can I do anything for you?"

"Yes, please. I'll come and let you in. It might take a while."

"Don't worry, I'm in no hurry."

As soon as I saw him it was obvious he was in a lot of pain.

"Oh dear, Ian. You're in a bad way. I feel terrible."

"Hey, you weren't to know," Ian said. He gestured for me to come in.

"But it was because of all the digging you did for me."

"No, Bert it wasn't. I have been away from the allotment, but that's because of work. This only happened a few days ago. Well, I say happened, actually I just woke up with it one morning."

"What has your doctor said?" I asked as I took a seat.

Ian stayed standing and took hold of the back of a chair. "I haven't seen him. Back pain is pretty common and there's nothing they can do."

"It is common, yes," I agreed. Even though retired, I was a bit hurt by his dismissive attitude to doctors.

"Bert, you asked if you could do anything for me. Would you mind fetching me some painkillers and milk?"

"That's no trouble." I was glad of the chance to do something to help.

"Would you get my wallet for me? It's in my briefcase in the corner. If you wouldn't mind taking my keys with you, I'll just go back to bed."

"Is that what you've been doing since the pain began?"

"Yes. It doesn't hurt so bad when I lie down and you're supposed to rest a bad back, aren't you?"

"That used to be the advice, but it's wrong. Often it's better to carry on with normal activities as much as possible."

"Oh."

From his expression I guessed he'd just remembered what I used to do for a living.

"I suppose I should have checked with the doctor."

"If you like, I'll take a look and check it is just simple lower back pain."

"It doesn't feel simple." Ian removed his dressing gown and turned his back to me.

After a quick examination and a few questions, I was sure Ian didn't have anything too serious wrong so I set off for the shops. I bought painkillers, milk, bread, cheese, apples and a carton of orange juice.

Back at his house I gave him two tablets and a cup of tea.

"Take two aspirin and call me in the morning?" he joked.

"Something like that. Give them a chance to work and then try walking about a bit. I've put a few things in your fridge, so get yourself something to eat. I'll be off down my allotment now, but I'll come back later and see how you are."

"Thanks, Bert."

Ian wasn't any worse when I returned. I'd taken some sweet peas that I'd grown

"Thanks, Bert, although I don't know what the neighbours will be thinking." He laughed and then winced.

"You don't want to laugh, it'll hurt your back," I warned a little too late. Before I left, I promised I'd keep an eye on his allotment.

A week later, Ian was back there himself. The first day he just walked around having a look at what needed doing, but soon he was weeding and tying in. A month later he was helping me out again instead of the other way round.

One day I was chatting to Malcolm about bindweed, when Ian approached

"My back feels fine now, Bert. I wouldn't want to go through that again though. Is there anything I can do to stop it recurring?"

"The general advice is to keep active. You don't need to do special exercises, just normal activities."

"Such as mowing the paths around your plot?" Malcolm suggested.

I laughed. "Exactly what the doctor ordered!"

It was good to have things back to normal.

19 Things Aren't Always As They Seem

Sophie scowled into the mirror, wondering if she dare leave her flat. This was her boring doctor's fault. He'd made so much fuss about sunburn being bad for her health, she'd gone for an all-over fake tan. She couldn't go out looking pasty. She'd never attract a decent bloke if she did. Typically though, the minute she tried to be sensible, it had gone horribly wrong. The colour had been great for the first few days, but it was going weird now.

There wasn't likely to be anyone much about at this time of day, Sophie assured herself, and anyone she did see would be rushing off to work and hopefully wouldn't notice her. She pulled on a long sleeved top, brushed her fair hair over her face and made a run for it. No one saw her on the way up to Mrs Jennings' flat. Sophie quickly slipped inside and rummaged through the old lady's cupboards.

It didn't take long for her to find the watering can. Tending the African violets took rather longer. There were hundreds of them. Not only were they squeezed on to every windowsill, but Mrs Jennings had glass shelves across the windows and those were jam packed with plants too. Sophie smiled at the way the plants were carefully arranged so the different mauve, purple and pink flowers blended together with just enough bright colours amongst the pastel ones to create contrast without looking gaudy. So different from the way Mrs Jennings looked herself.

Sophie didn't hang around in the empty flat. She'd have

been in a rush for work anyway, but now she'd have to spend longer than usual on her make-up sorting out her weird tan. It made her feel tired just to think about getting ready and running down to the bus stop. It really wasn't fair. She'd hardly drunk anything last night and she'd been home well before one, so why did she feel so lousy?

The problem was the tan. Her skin was itchy and felt hot. Looking at her yellowy complexion was making her feel a bit sick too. She'd be suing the salon, or maybe phoning one of the TV programmes that investigated con merchants, if they didn't put things right and refund her money pretty sharpish. Not that she wanted to be seen on TV, or anywhere else, with her awful tan.

Sophie wouldn't allow herself to think about being spotted by the man in the accounts department of the company where she was a marketeer. Harry was drop dead gorgeous and cooler than a vodka ice lolly. Too cool actually because he'd shown almost no interest in her, despite her subtle and not so subtle hints. Still, she hadn't entirely given up on him.

It wasn't just that she didn't want to be seen looking less than fabulous, she really was feeling rough. She'd better phone work.

"Sorry, but I won't be in today, Mike."

"Oh dear. Nothing too serious I hope?"

"Don't think so. I just feel a bit rough, you know? Probably a virus or something. I expect I'll be back on Monday."

"You look after yourself."

Sophie went back to bed. Maybe a few hours more sleep was all she needed?

By lunch-time, Sophie didn't feel any better and looked worse. She rang the surgery and made an emergency appointment. She dragged herself down to the surgery. Good thing Doctor 'call me Tim' Wilson was so boring, or she'd be feeling even sorrier for herself. He never exactly saw her at her best. He himself always looked pretty good, but he was sooo dull. A date with him must be like trying to rob a bank with a copper. Her every move would be criticised.

She glanced round the waiting room. Everyone else was either covered in horrible spots or coughing and sneezing. In comparison, maybe she didn't look so bad. Sophie managed to comb her hair and apply some lippy before she was called for her appointment.

"Hello, Sophie. What can I do for you today?"

She described her symptoms and added, "I don't think it can all be due to the tan."

"Neither do I. You look as though you're jaundiced."

"Is that bad?" She gave her most charming smile to encourage him to reassure her there was nothing bad about her. It didn't work. She must be losing her touch.

"That depends on the cause. It's a symptom of some liver conditions rather than an illness."

"Liver conditions?" Sophie had heard that drinking too much could be bad for the liver. Was he going to warn her, yet again, to cut down on the tequila slammers?

"I like a drink, but I know plenty of people who have a lot more and they're not ill."

Doctor Tim just gave her a look.

She gave him one right back as he told her off yet again

119

about her unhealthy lifestyle. The lecture wasn't as bad as it could have been, because Sophie was able to concentrate on his deep, sexy voice and daydream about him saying something far more interesting. At least, she could until he said he thought she'd contracted hepatitis B by having unprotected sex.

Doctor Tim arranged for her to have a blood test, gave her a leaflet about hepatitis and advised her on how to avoid passing on the infection. "Look after yourself a bit too, Sophie. Try to eat some fruit, get some fresh air and there's no need to stay away from work or your family once you feel well. Normal social contact is fine."

Sophie hoped she'd soon be feeling like a bit of normal social contact – and that she'd soon be looking normal enough for people to want to make contact with her.

She grinned at Doctor Wilson. He really wasn't a bad chap and he'd been right about the smoking. She didn't get so out of breath while dancing now and she'd saved enough cash for some fabulous shoes and matching bag. She bet those blue eyes of his would sparkle if she was to be able to tell him she'd not had a drink or cigarette since her last visit and instead had been eating vegetables. Would tomato sauce on her pizza count?

When she got home, Sophie discovered a postcard delivered to her by mistake. Whoever had written it was having such an exciting time in Sri Lanka it made Sophie tired just thinking about it so she went back to bed.

The following day, a large bouquet of flowers arrived from her work colleagues who'd all signed a get well card. Sophie looked to see if the good looking bloke from accounts had signed it. He had, 'Best wishes, Harry'. That was only slightly better than nothing which was what she'd got from all the other men she'd been in contact with recently. To be fair, they couldn't know she was ill because she didn't have their number to call them and they couldn't send flowers because they didn't know her address.

Mrs Jennings returned from her trip and called in on Sophie that evening.

"Hello dear, I just wanted to thank... oh my goodness, you've got jaundice!"

"Yeah. It's not catching though." Usually Sophie tried to keep conversations with her elderly neighbour to a minimum but today she wanted someone to talk to. Besides, just standing up was making her feel tired. "Come in."

Mrs Jennings fussed about tucking a throw around Sophie and making them both a cup of tea.

"Thanks, Mrs Jennings."

"Call me Gertie, dear."

Sophie gave a weak smile. Gertrude Jennings had repeatedly tried to make friends with Sophie. Today the old lady didn't look quite so odd. Probably because she wasn't wearing the bright red beret or cerise coat she usually had on when Sophie bumped into her. Without them to clash with, her hair seemed vibrant red rather than alarmingly ginger.

"So tell me about this," Mrs Jennings said, pointing at Sophie's yellow skin.

Sophie found herself crying as she explained. "I've been such an idiot. I thought I was being so cool and having fun by going out clubbing every night. When blokes took me back to their place I thought I was popular, but really everyone must think I'm such a tart." She shut up when she remembered who she was talking to. Old Gertrude Jennings must be so shocked to hear about Sophie's sex life.

Mrs Jennings laughed. "Oh dear, I know it isn't funny, Sophie, but you so remind me of myself when I realised the free love of the sixties was no such thing."

"But I..." Sophie really didn't know what to say.

"Don't get yourself in a state, dear. You have had fun in a way, but maybe now it's time to look for something different?"

Sophie nodded.

"Maybe one special man?"

"Yes. I would like that," she admitted.

"And you are very popular. Everyone in the building likes you and not just because you water our plants and replace light bulbs when we need a hand. And look at these lovely flowers." She picked up the card which Sophie had propped against them.

"They're just from work."

"Your colleagues put in enough money for lilies and roses and look at all the lovely comments saying how much you're missed."

Sophie smiled. Mrs Jennings was right, she probably had been missed. Sophie was bright and cheerful. It was good to have people like that around you.

"I've missed you too, er, Gertie. How was your holiday?" She couldn't remember where the old lady had said she was going because she'd not paid attention.

"Fantastic, dear. I got to scrub one of the babies with a

coconut."

"A coconut?" Sophie might not be the only one in need of medical help.

"Yes. Well, the outer husk. They really like being rubbed with them and lie down in the water to let you do it."

"Babies do?"

"Yes. I know they're still huge and tough looking, but really baby elephants are so cute. I'd have happily stayed in that stream for the whole fortnight."

"Right. Er, where was it you went again?"

"Sri Lanka. Didn't you get my postcard?"

"Oh! Yes."

Over the next few days, Gertie popped down regularly to make sure Sophie was OK and eating properly. They chatted about everything, even men. Gertie confided her interest in shy Alan from the bowls club and Sophie suggested toning down her colour scheme might make her seem more approachable.

"It worked, dear, he's asked me to lunch on Wednesday!"

"Brilliant! Any tips for attracting Harry when I get back to work?"

"What is he interested in?"

"Accounts." Sophie rolled her eyes.

"There's your trouble. If you're not interested in what he does, he probably doesn't know you're interested in him."

Gertie had a point, so when Sophie returned to work she asked Harry to explain his spreadsheets.

He said, "I'd be delighted to. Perhaps over a drink?"

The drink turned into several, followed by a visit to a way cool nightclub. She was easily persuaded to agree to another date.

There was more good news to come when Sophie returned to her doctor.

"The blood test confirmed you do only have hepatitis B, Sophie."

"Oh, thank you, Doctor, er, Tim."

"You're welcome."

She could tell he had more to say. "What is it?"

"I've asked Doctor Beatty to accept you as her patient."

"You're leaving?"

"No. I just feel it would be better if I wasn't your GP any longer."

"But why? You understand me and I do listen really. I gave up smoking and I only drink at the weekend and not that much really, even then and I eat vegetables and dancing is exercise..."

"Doctor Beatty is very nice. I'm sure you'll get on very well with her."

"Yes, but..." Except there wasn't anything else she could say.

There was no getting away from it, Sophie was hurt. OK, Doctor Beatty was probably fine medically and at least Sophie wouldn't keep getting falsely high blood pressure readings when it was her hands, not Doctor Tim's on her arm. She wasn't really bothered by his startlingly blue eyes and lovely smile, but that didn't mean she wanted to be rejected by him.

Sophie called in on Gertie that evening.

"I don't get it. I always thought he was nice and cared about me, even if he did go on a bit. Good thing Harry is being so nice to me, or I could get a complex."

"It's going well with Harry?" Gertie asked.

"Oh yes, he's great."

"So why have you started smoking again?"

"Well, he does and he says he feels guilty if I don't."

"You're drinking more too, aren't you?"

"A bit maybe. He's very generous."

"Things aren't always as they seem, Sophie," Gertie said.

Sophie thought about that as she got ready to go out. She hadn't minded the older lady asking about her smoking and drinking because she knew she was just concerned, not trying to be a killjoy. The hepatitis infection might not have been the disaster it had first seemed. Maybe she should try to see it as a warning to take more care of her health.

When she met Harry at the club, she asked for an orange juice to drink. That seemed sensible to her, cutting her alcohol intake and increasing her fruit consumption in one stroke.

"Right, orange and what?" Harry asked.

"Just orange."

"Oh come on, Sophie. Don't be boring."

"I'm not, I just fancy an orange juice, oh and by the way, I've quit smoking again."

"What? I thought you were fun, but obviously I got that wrong."

Sophie didn't bother explaining she'd also decided to stop having unprotected sex. Clearly he was more interested in what he wanted than in her health. She got a taxi home and had an early night.

The following morning she had a clear head and was out of bed in plenty of time to get ready for work – and to collect her post and read it before racing for the train. There was just one letter. It was from Doctor Tim. In it he explained his reason for asking her to transfer to another GP. While she had been his patient it would have been unethical to ask her out. Things were different now, so did she fancy a curry?

She texted her acceptance to the number he'd provided before rushing upstairs to see Gertie.

"You were right, things weren't as they seemed with Harry, or Tim."

"I know dear. Neither were they with you. When I first moved in here it seemed you were self-centred. I soon discovered that wasn't true. In fact I think it's taken until now for you to really care about yourself."

20 Please Remember Me

"So from despatch it's just up one floor to the gym." The lady stepped out the lift into the most luxurious looking fitness suite Vivian had ever seen. "Oh good, there are some people your age here. This is Lucy, she's in accounts. I'm sure you'll get on, especially if you like silly jokes."

Vivian shook hands with Lucy, just as she had with everyone she'd been introduced to that morning, before being taken over to meet another girl who was apparently a computer whizz. Vivian doubted she'd remember a single name.

"Sorry," her guide said as they returned to the lift. "I'm overloading you with information, aren't I?"

Relieved, Vivian nodded. "It was a long flight and I am a bit tired to take it all in," she admitted.

"Not to worry, I'll escort you back to your accommodation and you can settle in. I'm afraid I'm so enthusiastic about our wonderful facilities I get carried away. Let's walk through the courtyard; it's beautiful."

Vivian looked through the huge glass doors and gasped. 'Courtyard' and 'beautiful' were both understatements. Before them was a huge tropical garden.

"You're welcome to come out here whenever you like of course, but I strongly advise you not to spend too long out in the sun."

As soon as they stepped outside, Vivian could see why. The temperature was very high, even when they passed through the shade of the lush planting. Every leaf and flower seemed too perfect to be real, from the fabulous scarlet and burgundy amaryllis blooms almost erupting from the ground at her feet to the cerise and mandarin bougainvillaea scrambling like the most gorgeous of sunsets up into the sky. The bright colours and exotic scents made Vivian's head swim. The reassuring hum of the air conditioning was very welcome as they entered the accommodation block.

"Here we are, back at your room."

"Thank you... Paula." Only just in time, Vivian recalled her name.

Paula grinned. "You're welcome. I'll meet you in the lobby at nine tomorrow morning as I've probably got you so confused you won't remember where your office is."

Vivian laughed at the truth of that, let herself into her apartment, lay on the bed and closed her eyes.

When she awoke a few hours later, Vivian felt just as disorientated as she had during her whirlwind tour of the complex. It wasn't a new sensation; for days now her life had taken on a dreamlike quality. It had started with her seeing the job advertisement. It sounded perfect for her; she'd always wanted to travel and possessed all the required qualifications and experience.

She'd downloaded the application form, completed it and emailed it back immediately. The following morning she'd been called and offered an interview. It had lasted more than two hours and left her feeling they knew her better than she knew herself.

"We need someone who can start almost immediately, are you in that position?"

She'd assured them she was and went home to pack up her life. It hadn't taken long. Her friends took her for drinks, wished her well and almost concealed their envy. She'd got a taxi to the airport. No one waved her off, but Paula had been waiting in Bermuda to collect her.

Vivian checked her watch. It was still early evening, plenty of time for her to take a look round and get something to eat from the restaurant. She found her way back to the courtyard and wandered around the exotic space enjoying the fragrance that wafted down from the oleander trees and twining jasmine.

Iridescent dragonflies flitted overhead and butterflies seemed to dance before her, leading her around the garden. A huge one with burnished orange wings laced with black sunk down on to her outstretched hand. It reminded Vivian of delicate stained glass. The butterfly rose, then dipped down to rest on a discreet sign saying 'library'. Soon she noticed that although all the doorways looked the same, each was neatly labelled with signs set into the flower beds. Vivian needn't have worried about getting lost.

After a lap of the garden she'd learned there was a pool, health centre and cinema on site. The complex was more like a holiday resort than working environment. Soon she felt hungry and headed for the restaurant.

Three girls invited Vivian to join them. She recognised one, but couldn't recall her name or in which department she'd worked. Vivian glanced down the menu, dazzled by the choice. A waiter persuaded her to try swordfish with lime dressing and accompany it with a glass of chardonnay.

"Oh, I didn't ask how much it costs," she exclaimed as he sauntered away.

The girl who looked familiar laughed. "Easy to tell you're new here! Staff don't pay, silly. I'm Sue by the way, that's Georgette and Natasha."

The food was excellent and the girls chatted easily over the meal. At least, three of them did. Natasha, who was extremely pale, seemed distracted and hardly spoke until she offered to walk Vivian back to her room.

As they left the restaurant, Natasha clung to Vivian's arm as though she was scared they'd get separated in the courtyard. She didn't say anything until they reached Vivian's apartment.

"Do you have anything to write with?"

"Of course."

"Write down my name and details then." She pushed her way in and was very insistent.

She relaxed a little as Vivian wrote down the information on an envelope. "I'll be going soon and I want to be sure I won't be forgotten."

Vivian suggested those who'd been there longer would be more likely to remember her.

"It's too late once you've been here for a while."

"Well, I won't forget you," Vivian said. She certainly wouldn't, but neither would she wish to contact such an oddball. As soon as Natasha left, she screwed up the envelope and threw it away.

The next morning, Vivian made sure she was waiting nice

and early for Paula. When Vivian went down to the lobby she found Georgette reading a book. The author's name was familiar, one of Vivian's favourites, but the cover wasn't, so perhaps it was a new release.

"I don't think I've read that one," Vivian said.

"It's really good, his best so far, I think. I got it from the library, so you'll be able to have it when I'm done."

"Great, thanks."

Paula arrived then and took Vivian away. As they walked, she asked about Natasha.

"Sorry, I can't think who you might mean. Staff turnover is pretty high as most people, like yourself, are only here for short postings. It's difficult to keep up."

Vivian felt better hearing that. Her own short contract must be normal then, not a sign they hadn't really wanted her. She soon settled into the work and often shared her evening meal with Sue and Georgette. When Vivian mentioned Natasha they pulled faces and made gestures to suggest the girl was unstable.

Vivian said, "Yeah I thought she seemed strange." They didn't talk about her again.

Every morning, as she left the accommodation block, Vivian passed Georgette. They chatted for a minute or two and Georgette told Vivian which page she was on.

"Sorry I'm such a slow reader."

After a week, Vivian didn't see Georgette again, although she did find the book in the library.

"Georgette finished it eventually, then?" she asked the assistant.

"Sorry, don't know who you mean."

"She borrowed the book before me."

The assistant shrugged. "Must have been before my time."

But hadn't the library assistant already been there when Vivian started? It was so hard to remember as nobody seemed to stay in the same office for long. Oh well, if Georgette was such a slow reader she wouldn't have borrowed many books so maybe it wasn't surprising the librarian didn't remember her. Vivian asked a few other people, but no one seemed to know who she was talking about. Vivian realised her description was very vague and though she tried, she couldn't remember any helpful details about Georgette's appearance.

A week later, Vivian walked over to Sue's department at lunchtime to suggest they go to the gym before dinner. Sue had vanished. Her computer was on, a half-eaten chocolate bar lay abandoned on her desk and her bag hung over the back of her chair. Her colleagues were concerned and had begun a search which Vivian joined in. Soon a manager arrived.

"There's no need to panic, people. Look, it's a lovely day, why don't you take the afternoon off and go to the pool? Best not go sunbathing though, it's even hotter than usual out there."

"We can't just go," Vivian said.

"Of course you can. I'll stay here and take care of things," she said.

The disappearance reminded her of something, Vivian thought, but she didn't know what. She thought it might have something to do with Georgette, whoever Georgette was.

There wasn't time to worry about that though because Paula introduced her to Sonia. "She's new here, so I was hoping you'd take her under your wing a bit. Look after her. This place can be a bit confusing at first."

"Of course I will. Actually it's not just at first this place is confusing. Only this morning I thought I was headed for despatch and ended up in the health centre. Then I had to try and convince the doctor I was fine!"

Paula laughed. "Well, I *think* I'm leaving you in good hands, Sonia."

Sonia was fun to take around. She was amazed the restaurant was free and that she could leave her desk anytime she liked to go swimming or to stroll in the garden. She wanted to know the names of the flowers, making Vivian wish she knew them. Vivian enjoyed surprising her with all the wonderful facilities they had in the complex. They arranged to meet in the courtyard the next day, so Vivian could explain about the almost hidden signs.

Sonia was late, so Vivian found a comfortable spot in the shade to wait. The heat must have made her doze off because she woke with a start and remembered Sue's disappearance. How could she have forgotten that? She raced over to her office. Sue wasn't there. There were no empty desks although Vivian was almost sure they'd been moved around. Everyone was working calmly.

"Where's Sue?" Vivian asked the person whose desk was closest to where her friend's used to be.

"Sorry, don't know her."

"She worked right there, near the window."

The girl shrugged. "Did she? Sorry, but I'm new."

The manager arrived. "Are you all right, Vivian?"

"No. I was looking for my friend and she's gone."

"Don't worry, I'll take you to her." The lady escorted Vivian to the courtyard where Sonia was waiting for her.

"Sorry, I didn't mean to worry you by wandering off, but I found the signs you told me about and I followed one saying cinema. There's a great film about to start, let's go see it."

Vivian nodded. The cinema would be cool and the heat and humidity in the garden was making her feel faint. She enjoyed the film and felt much better after watching it. As soon as they stepped outside she felt ill again so they rushed into the restaurant. For the next few days, Vivian made sure she stayed inside. The complex completely surrounded the courtyard, so there was never any need to go outside unless she wanted to. The gentle sound of the air conditioning soothed her and she forgot her worries. Or nearly all her worries because it seemed she was forgetting too much.

The doctor examined Vivian and assured her there was nothing physically wrong.

"Then it's a psychological problem," Vivian said.

"What is?" she asked.

"I keep forgetting things. Silly things I'm sure I should know."

"Really? I've checked your work record and it's excellent."

Vivian was unable to provide an example of the things she'd forgotten so couldn't persuade the doctor there was anything wrong. Forgetting her dislike of the heat, Vivian stepped out into the courtyard. She soon realised her mistake. There! That was proof she forgot things. She'd keep a diary of these details to show the doctor.

The shop in the complex didn't sell diaries, or notebooks or writing paper. The woman at the counter was surprised anyone would want them. So was everyone else when she asked if they would give her any spare paper they had.

"Use your computer instead, it's much better."

"Yes do. The boss doesn't mind."

Vivian couldn't remember the boss's name or what he looked like. She should know, shouldn't she? She ran to her apartment, repeating 'boss's name, boss's name' to herself. She wrote the phrase on her arm as soon as she could find a pen. For some reason, it was stuffed right at the back of her drawer with scrunched up pieces of paper. On each of these was written a name and a few brief details of the person. Vivian had no idea who Sue, Paula, Natasha or Georgette were, but it seemed she'd known them at one time. People left the company all the time, she knew that. Nobody ever said goodbye or mentioned their contract was coming to an end. She understood that with so many staff changes they wouldn't have constant parties and collections, but surely some people would say something?

She picked up the phone and asked to be put through to the boss. Once connected she tried to explain her concerns.

"Vivian, don't upset yourself so. Come up and we'll talk about this."

"Thank you."

As Vivian replaced the handset she realised she didn't actually know where his office was. She had to go out into the courtyard and check the signs, then get up there as quickly as she could. It wasn't surprising she arrived hot and flustered. Fortunately, the air conditioning in his waiting room was even better than that in her own block. The low pitched humming noise it made was a bit more noticeable, but it was a soothing sound and Vivian soon began to relax. The boss would be able to sort everything out.

When Vivian was ushered in to see him she marvelled at the lovely views.

"I hadn't realised your office was so high up or that we were so near the sea."

"Can I offer you a drink to enjoy whilst you admire the scenery?"

She whirled around, worried she'd been rude but the boss just smiled and held up a bowl of fruit and a glass. He made her smoothie himself, complimenting her on her on the great work she'd been doing as he produced a beautiful and delicious fruity cocktail.

"So, what was it you wanted to see me about?"

She'd been worried about something. It had seemed important. Silly to be worried when everything was so lovely and the boss was so nice. He wouldn't let anything bad happen.

"About people leaving, I think you said?"

People did leave. Yes, that was it. She'd been worried that a lot of people had left.

"Don't worry, we won't overwork you. New staff will be starting soon."

She hadn't worried about being overworked. Nobody ever had to work very hard, not as far as she could remember. She shook her head. It was hard to explain, but it was something about them going that worried her.

"This is a very popular posting, so we have to keep the contracts short to give lots of people the chance to come."

Yes, that made sense. Something hadn't though, if only she could explain.

"Someone left something behind." She was almost sure she'd seen a bag abandoned over the back of a chair.

"We get visitors from other departments. People often leave things behind. My theory is they like it here so much they want an excuse to come back."

Vivian smiled as he laughed at his own joke. It was a relief to have an answer.

"What happens to the things they leave?"

"We send them on, of course."

It all made sense and Vivian wanted to write down that there was nothing to worry about before she forgot why everything was really OK. She asked the boss if he'd mind her doing that.

"It's a paperless office, Vivian. But feel free to use my computer to send yourself a message."

Vivian gratefully sat at his desk and logged on. Because it wasn't her usual terminal, her whole profile flashed up on the screen. Vivian saw that her contract end date had been brought forward.

"Why do I have to leave early?" she asked. "You said my work was good and I didn't mean to cause trouble..."

"Shh, it's all right. You're not going early. That's the date that was agreed."

"No. I had longer. I'm almost sure I had longer."

"Wishful thinking, Vivian. I can understand you wanting to stay on, but I'm afraid it's not possible."

As instructed she checked the computer records, including the email offering her the job. They all matched. So that's why she couldn't remember things – she hadn't wanted to because that would mean she'd remember she had to leave. She was going soon and everyone would forget all about her. She didn't want to be forgotten.

Vivian returned to her apartment. On the landing, she saw a new girl being given a set of keys and told to go in and unpack and that soon someone would come along soon to show her round. Vivian listened at her own door until she was sure there was no one outside, then slipped out and knocked on the new girl's door.

"Hi, I'm Vivian. Do you have anything to write with?"

"Of course," the new girl said.

"Write down my name and details then." She pushed her way in and was very insistent.

Vivian relaxed a little as the girl wrote down the information she gave. "I'll be going soon and I want to be sure I won't be forgotten."

The new girl kept her distance, frowned and suggested those who'd been there longer would be more likely to remember Vivian.

"It's too late once you've been here for a while."

"Well, I won't forget you, er, Vivian," the girl said.

As Vivian left the apartment she thought she heard the sound of scrunching paper over the soft hum of the air conditioning.

21 Other Stories

We couldn't find a parking space close to Max Gate, home of author Thomas Hardy, but as desperate situations call for desperate remedies, we abandoned our car under the greenwood tree.

My husband said, "It will be safe here, far from the madding crowd, protected from prying eyes by the woodlanders."

"I'd rather leave it in the care of our fellow townsmen," I remarked but as usual he wasn't really listening.

He strode on ahead of me, the well beloved husband of mine. I followed more slowly, lost in thought; I'm an imaginative woman. I knew there was to be a reading and wondered if we'd hear extracts from *Jude the Obscure* or *Tess of the d'Urbevilles*.

I took a wrong turning and ended up in an extremely dark lane, populated by thrushes and other creatures. Fortunately there were moments of vision when I thought I might see friends beyond. During one, my gaze was met by a pair of blue eyes and I realised I was interrupting a tryst at an ancient earthwork! It rather reminded me of our exploits at West Poley, so I just pretended not to notice and hurried on in search of my husband. I saw him ahead and began the pursuit of the well beloved.

When I found him he was a changed man!

"My dear, you're a woman much missed," he said before returning his attention to his companions.

He was listening intently to the Wessex tales they told. He was in serious discussion with a vicar, a woman dressed in tweed and a rather military looking gentleman. I soon learned these were not the three strangers I at first took them to be. One was the trumpet major my husband bought our car from, the woman was part of a group of noble dames who arranged flowers at our local church and the distracted preacher was the very man who conducted our wedding service. I was about to remind him of that when I recalled his reaction to our informal wedding photos. Us two on a tower was, apparently, not very funny.

"What's wrong?" I enquired.

I was told that Mr Duke, who is the mayor of Casterbridge, and his wife had vanished. "The poor man and the lady took a stroll down the lane and haven't been seen for some time."

"Not to worry," I reassured them all. "It's one of life's little ironies that I myself got lost on the same lane. I'm sure they'll be back after a mere interlude."

I was correct and after the reappearance of Mr and Mrs Duke we all went inside Max Gate to listen to a reading. Appropriately, or so I felt, we heard a passage from *Return of the Native*.

Whether you believe my story or consider it no more than a few satires of circumstance, I assure you it's true – and all written by the hand of Ethelberta.

22 Watching

Number 42 had an expensive car displayed out front and all kinds of tempting electricals visible through patio doors at the back. Some people might as well put up signs inviting you to help yourself, Mitch thought. Getting in might be difficult. There were lights front and back and a shiny red box, indicating a newly installed alarm system. Still you couldn't go by that, sometimes people got careless. They didn't always bother to set alarms. Lights were easy too, he'd been told. Just needed an enterprising person to set them off a few times. The householder blamed a neighbour's cat and went back to the television.

Mitch fancied driving the magnificent machine sat on the driveway and who wouldn't want that stereo? It wasn't worth the risk. He didn't want to end up down the police station answering awkward questions.

Might as well make things easy for himself and choose number 38. It had poor security all round and a low rear fence allowing a quick getaway. Large shrubs at the front provided cover and there was a bin conveniently close to the back gate. The old lady also looked as though she'd be easy to deal with; Mitch could be very persuasive.

Checking he was unobserved, Mitch slipped behind a shrub – luckily nothing thorny. It was easy to make his way toward the side gate. No light was triggered. No dog barked. He edged toward a window and glanced in. There was no lock, so he could easily open it. He didn't know if the owner was home though. Better check.

Mitch approached the front door. No hallway light showed, so he peered through the letter box. Bingo! A big bunch of keys lay on the hallway table. A small hook on a stick would soon mean Mitch could drive away in the car. It wasn't much of a car; no match for the one at number 42.

Mitch returned his attention to the job in hand. He wasn't here to enter the property. Just to find out as much as he could and report back.

"Don't do anything, lad, but think it through as though you were about to do the job. How would you get in? What might stop you, what could you easily take? Is it worth the risk?"

"Yes, I remember, and if I get spotted I'll do what you said. Keep calm and speak with authority," Mitch had replied.

"That's right; we'll come back tomorrow after you've done all the preparation."

Remembering his instructions, Mitch climbed on to the bin and dropped into the back garden. He walked cautiously down the side path. Just as well because otherwise he'd have banged his shin on the ladder. A ladder! No need to bother carrying tools about when your 'customers' provided them for you.

Mitch stepped out behind the house. Again, no security lights triggered. Every window was in darkness. One was open.

Mitch considered how he'd burgle the property. He'd check there were no lights on, just as he'd done tonight.

Then he'd walk right up to the front door and knock. If anyone was home, he'd ask if they'd like to welcome Jesus into their life. He'd be gone in moments. If the coast was clear, he'd put the ladder against the wall, enter through the open window and get what he could. Maybe then he'd use the home owner's car to get away.

Once he'd seen enough, Mitch reported back. "Security is very weak."

"So, we go back tomorrow?"

"Of course."

The following evening, the two men walked boldly to the front door and knocked. After a moment a light went on, shortly afterwards the door was opened.

"Good evening, madam," Mitch said and held out his identification. "We are police officers and would like to offer you some home security advice."

23 Grapefruit

Dale sighed as he emptied the bag of kitchen waste on to the compost heap. All that grapefruit skin couldn't be good. Surely it would make it too acid? He worried that might affect the growth of his prize winning lettuce. Oh well, if they helped Erica he could put up with it. Maybe adding limestone would help? There was usually a way round any problem if you looked for it.

As Dale went inside, the smell of grapefruit hit him anew. When his sister Daphne visited, she always remarked on the lovely, fresh citrus fragrance of the house, but she didn't have to smell the rotten peel-ridden things day in day out. Oh well, it had been his suggestion.

"I've put on so much weight," Erica said a few months ago.

She was heavier, it was true. Mainly as a result of breaking her ankle. Naturally she couldn't get out and about for a while. That meant she got bored and spent a lot of time snacking in front of the TV. He'd not said anything as he'd assumed once she was mobile again she'd go back to her old ways and lose the weight.

It hadn't worked out like that. As all her clothes were too tight she'd felt self-conscious going out and she'd got used to the sugary treats. She stayed in and ate more. Other than work, where she sat down all day, Erica rarely left the house.

Dale didn't mind her being bigger, but he could see it was making her unhappy and knew, if the cycle continued, she'd damage her health.

He'd hugged her. "It's only because of your ankle, love. A bit of exercise and healthy eating will sort that out."

"I can't show myself at an exercise class looking like this, besides I'm so unfit I wouldn't be able to do it."

Dale rather thought she was missing the point of the classes, but didn't argue. If she was feeling down she'd need to know he was on her side.

"How about a walk down the allotment with me? We could pick some lettuce for tea." He was eager for her to admire his neat rows of Cos, Little Gem and Red Salad Bowl.

He thought she was going to refuse, but eventually she nodded.

"Put one of my work shirts on, to keep yourself clean." She wasn't going to get dirty picking lettuce, but his shirts were big and baggy, so she'd hopefully feel comfortable in them.

Dale was quite alarmed by how red faced and puffed out Erica got, just from the ten minute walk and stooping to gather leaves. Seeing her every day he'd not really noticed how unfit she'd got. When he saw her smile the following morning he got another jolt. He hadn't appreciated just how unhappy she'd been either.

"I think I've lost a pound! Thanks for helping, Dale."

Erica made a salad to take for her lunch that day and walked down the allotment with him that evening. She picked lettuce as Dale sowed a fresh row. She ate salad for her tea and packed more for work. His plan was working perfectly and if she continued eating lettuce at this rate he could easily justify buying seeds of Iceberg, Lollo Rosso and maybe some of those really pale butterheads to add to his collection.

All was well until the weekend when she joined him in eating a huge portion of fish and chips.

"I know I shouldn't, but if you're having that I can't sit and eat nothing but salad."

Dale, determined not to add to her problems, said, "I'll eat the same as you if that will help." Growing lettuce was his passion, but he was quite happy to eat it too.

"It would, but that won't be enough for you."

"I can have bigger portions and still have my usual lunch in the canteen at work."

Much as he liked eating the fresh produce he'd grown, Dale soon began to see why Erica had been tempted by a fish supper. Without any dressing, cheese or thick wedges of bread and butter, lettuce started to seem a bit dull after a few days, especially as he had rather a glut of the flabby leaved oak-leaf type and his new, more interesting selections weren't ready yet. Compared with the things she'd got used to eating recently, a plate of leaves, however fresh and crunchy, must seem very bland. Fool that he was, he'd suggested grapefruit. It had seemed perfect; low calorie, healthy and tangy.

The grapefruit had worked very well for a while. Even Dale started losing weight, because once he got used to its flavour, the sugary snacks and puddings he'd been used to eating at work tasted far too sweet. Erica looked healthier and happier and lost a few pounds. It was slow going though, especially as she still didn't feel ready for any exercise other than their short walks.

They had grapefruit for breakfast, either fresh or as juice. Erica took some for her lunch. Tea always had either a grapefruit starter, grapefruit in the salad or grapefruit and mandarins as dessert. Quite often it was also accompanied by a glass of grapefruit juice. Actually it was only Dale who was fed up with the grapefruit. Erica was as enthusiastic as a religious convert. Oh well, it wouldn't be forever and seeing his wife optimistic again was worth a slight overdose of grapefruit. He did wonder what would be the human equivalent of gardener's limestone and if they should be eating it to counteract the grapefruit. He hadn't dared mention lime though, in case Erica added yet more citrus to their diet.

Dale rinsed the kitchen waste bucket and put it back in place.

"Phew, looks hot out there," Erica said.

"It is. How about we walk down town and treat ourselves to an ice cream?"

"No need. I have something better; grapefruit sorbet!"

"Maybe I'll just have a cold drink."

"I'll pour you some juice, love."

"It's OK, I'll just get some water." He hurried away with his glass before she could suggest ice and a slice – of grapefruit!

Dale picked up his Kindle, intending to sit in the shade and read. He'd recently downloaded a book about providing the optimum soil conditions for various crops. He wanted to check if he should omit the grapefruit skins from his compost heap.

The Kindle felt a bit sticky. A careful inspection revealed the screen was speckled with an unknown substance. Odd. Not so odd when he saw the book which automatically opened; a recipe book featuring a huge number of uses for grapefruit. Clearly Erica had been reading it while eating her favourite fruit and sprayed zest on the screen as she peeled, and juice from her fingers had transferred itself to the cover. Something had to be done!

When Erica thought she'd lost sufficient weight and gained a little fitness she intended to take up exercise classes. Once she did that she'd start losing weight in earnest. When that happened she could go back to eating normally. The answer was simple. Dale headed for the bathroom and made a slight adjustment to the scales.

The following morning Erica danced about the house in excitement at her weight loss. That evening she told him she'd felt light enough to use the stairs at work instead of taking the lift.

"I stopped to get my breath back halfway, but I did it."

"Brilliant, love. You're walking faster too."

"I think so. Oh that reminds me, I got something a little different for us to snack on as a treat to celebrate my weight loss."

To Dale, eating snacks didn't seem the ideal way to celebrate losing weight, but he was so pleased at the idea of something different to eat he kept the thought to himself.

"Look at these beauties!" Erica said holding up a big bag of grapefruit.

"They don't look much different to me."

"Not on the outside, but inside they're bright pink!"

"Oh… good."

Dale adjusted the scales again that night. He also called his sister Daphne to make a suggestion about the gift Erica would like for her birthday.

"Oh that's lovely!" Erica said when she unwrapped the flower print dress. Her cheerful smile suffered a slight setback when she looked at the label.

"Try it on," Dale urged.

"Please do, Erica. I'd love to see how it looks on you," Daphne added.

Their efforts were rewarded with a shriek of joy from Erica. "I haven't been able to get into this size for ages."

"You've done so well with your diet," Daphne said. "You're a real inspiration to me. How about we do exercise classes together? I couldn't face it on my own, but with you there..."

Erica was easily persuaded. The classes, combined with her lettuce and grapefruit rich diet soon meant she could wear other dresses marked the same size as her birthday gift, and do it without anyone needing to switch the labels first.

Six months later, Erica was lively, cheerful and weighed less than she had before her ankle injury.

"I'm so proud of you, love," Dale said when she was named slimmer of the year and interviewed for the local paper. He was too. Secretly he was a little proud of himself. The paper had included a small picture of 'the supportive husband growing salad leaves'. Although he himself seemed slightly out of focus, the rows of lettuce he posed amongst had come out a treat.

Everything seemed perfect until he suggested Erica might now like to make a change to her eating habits. Slightly less lettuce and a lot less grapefruit was his idea.

"Don't be silly, Dale. If it wasn't for the grapefruit I'd still be fat, miserable and unfit. Besides, I got this." She handed him a letter.

A consortium of grapefruit importers had seen the piece in the paper and asked if they could use her photo and story in their advertising. Erica had agreed and in exchange they'd promised her a lifetime's supply of big, juicy grapefruit.

Oh well. At least he'd found a use for all those skins. They were great at trapping the slugs and keeping them off the lettuce.

24 In The Eye Of The Beholder

Cecilia blinked as the early morning sun fell on her face. She pulled shut the huge oak door of her house, being careful not to leave an unsightly mark on the highly polished door knocker. She slipped on sunglasses in the hope it would make her less recognisable to the paparazzi and draped her cashmere shawl over her shoulders as she sauntered elegantly down the worn granite steps. As Cecilia negotiated the cobbled driveway, which swept down to the road, she didn't teeter at all on her designer heels. In just a couple of minutes she rounded the corner and took her place in the queue for the bus.

She took her usual seat; one of the sideways ones near the front so she could look at people further down the bus without it being obvious she was observing them. He was there again! 'The man on the bus' as she'd imaginatively named him. She grinned at him.

He was a scriptwriter using the public transport system in order to research inner-city dialogue. He must have a wonderful memory as he never took notes, but Cecilia could tell he was taking in every word of the conversations going on around him. He would have liked to talk to her of course, but couldn't until he'd finished collecting background material. Then he would make her the heroine of his film.

Cecilia made it into work only just on time. The boss stood by Cecilia's desk looking at his watch. Cecilia blinked.

Her boss broke into a broad smile and congratulated her for her excellent timekeeping. Cecilia blinked again and he dumped a heap of files on her desk.

"This lot are urgent, Cecilia. I need them finished today."

Oh well, Cecilia could fantasise but her boss would always see her as unfocussed and would never understand why she needed to catch the bus that, if all went well, got her to work just on time. How could she explain she was in love with a fellow passenger? Anyone who knew her would know she'd never be brave enough to do more than look and daydream about what might happen if they got together.

After three and a half hours in front of the computer, Cecilia stopped work and opened her lunch box. She blinked and then looked in at the tempting crusty rolls with camembert and cranberry jelly, garnished with watercress. Her mouth watered as she imagined the rich texture of the cheese and tang of the cranberries. To follow there was fruit salad. The exotic aroma of which was enough to make her briefly think of a lush forest somewhere warm and humid. Cecilia ate quickly; she had a lot of work to do and would need to continue through her break if she hoped to catch the right bus home.

At ten past five, Cecilia grabbed her mac and ran. Thankfully she'd worn flat pumps that morning and was able to get to the bus stop with seconds to spare. The man on the bus was there as usual. She smiled at the shy millionaire who she knew was looking for people in need to help.

He would have liked to buy her lavish gifts and take her to wonderful places but could see she didn't need the money and he's so insecure he couldn't see she'd appreciate him for more than his money and together they could give it all away and live a happy, normal life together.

Cecilia got off the bus and walked the short distance to her home. Outside the building she blinked then walked down a weathered brick path, under rose covered arches, breathing in the intoxicating scent of jasmine, stocks and lavender. She continued towards her thatched cottage until she reached the dainty white door with black painted iron fixtures. She unlocked it to reveal a room beautifully decorated in chintz fabrics and pastel patterned papers.

She mixed herself a cocktail and wondered where she'd go and what she'd do that evening. So many choices! Cecilia blinked and placed her orange squash next to a book she'd started reading. She'd have a quiet evening in and read that.

The next morning, after breakfast, Cecilia picked up her handbag and blinked. She left her light, spacious minimalist apartment, the silvers and greys of which perfectly toned with her sleek appearance, and glided down to street level in the glass elevator.

She only risked quick, furtive glances and the briefest flash of a smile at the man on bus. He was an undercover agent on the trail of dangerous terrorists and she didn't want to give the game away. He was keeping the country safe but doing it all for her. He'd like to talk to her of course but couldn't risk his professional integrity. Getting too close to her might compromise the success of his mission. Once it's over he'd make his feelings known.

Cecilia had another busy day of what at first appeared to be another pile of boring data input. She stared hard at the mountain of paperwork, blinked and discovered it was really an interesting and fulfilling, highly confidential task.

Lunch, after she'd blinked to clear eyes tired from staring at her screen, was revealed to be warm ciabatta bread oozing with cambozola cheese and decorated with zingy rocket leaves. To follow was a light fruit compote bursting with autumn flavours.

At ten to five, Cecilia's boss thanked her for working so hard and said she could go a little early. She blinked but he was still there smiling and gesturing to the door. Cecilia thanked him, put on her red mac and walked slowly to the bus stop. Too fast and she'd risk arriving in time for the earlier bus. She timed it right and got on the correct one.

He was there again, the man on the bus. Cecilia beamed at him. He was an eco campaigner, which is why he always used public transport. He was going to save the planet and make it a better place for her and the children they'd have together. He'd come over and speak to her but... There was no reason was there? She saw him every morning and smiled. If he was interested he could have moved down the bus and said hello.

Cecilia got off the bus and walked home. She didn't bother to blink away the tears filling her eyes. She climbed the dark smelly staircase, as the lift was out of order again, and let herself into her dingy flat. The highlight of the evening was packing her boring cheese sandwich, apple and banana as usual for lunch the next day.

The following morning Cecilia kept her eyes wide open and head high as she boarded the bus. She forced herself to smile as usual. He, the man on the bus, looked very sheepish as he returned her smile. Instantly she saw why; he was holding a crimson rose. He must have a girlfriend or at least someone he liked and was taking it to her. Cecilia blinked furiously but the rose was still there in his hand.

As soon as bus pulled away from the stop before hers, the man on the bus stood and walked towards her. She looked away to avoid embarrassment as he reached her.

"Here, I..."

She barely caught his mumble, but glanced at him just long enough to see he was offering her the rose. Cecilia blinked and saw he was blushing a darker red even than the perfect bloom. She took it just as the bus jolted to a halt and the doors wheezed open.

"Thanks!" she called as she leapt out.

It was sheer luck Cecilia got to work at all as she wasn't aware of where she was going. No amount of luck could get her there on time though. Her boss was waiting by Cecilia's desk, looking pointedly at his watch. His glare melted to a smile. Cecilia blinked but her boss was still smiling.

"What's that?" he gestured to the rose.

She explained about the man on the bus and admitted he was the reason she didn't always arrive at work on time.

"I'll let you off this time, but maybe you could suggest you both get an earlier one from now on?"

Cecilia nodded doubtfully. "I will, just as soon as I get the nerve to actually speak to him."

Her boss laughed. "Fair enough, but don't take too long about it."

At lunchtime she dumped her ordinary sandwiches and went out to buy nicer ones and pick up colour charts. Her small flat would look much better with a lick of paint in a cheerful shade. On the way she passed a bridal shop and stopped. Cecilia positioned herself so her reflection seemed to be wearing the hugely fabulous dress displayed there.

She blinked and her waist shrank to fit the dress, her hair fell lustrous around her shoulders and tasteful jewellery glinted from her ears, neck and fingers. Her father, suddenly taller and with more hair than when she'd seen him last week was walking her down the aisle towards the man on the bus. All around, cameras flashed and hundreds of adoring people gasped at her amazing beauty.

Cecilia blinked again and she was an ordinary looking girl, slightly plump but with nice eyes. She wasn't famous or rich or engaged but she had a few good friends, an OK job, nice family and there was a man who liked her enough to overcome his shyness and give her a rose. Her daydreams weren't going to stop, but from now on she was going to enjoy reality too.

Thank you for reading this book. I hope you enjoyed it. If you did, I'd really appreciate it if you could leave a short review on Amazon and/or Goodreads.

To learn more about my writing life, hear about new releases and get a free short story, sign up to my newsletter – https://mailchi.mp/677f65e1ee8f/sign-up or you can find the link on my website patsycollins.uk

More books by Patsy Collins

Novels –

Firestarter
Escape To The Country
A Year And A Day
Paint Me A Picture
Leave Nothing But Footprints
Acting Like A Killer

Non-fiction –

From Story Idea To Reader
(co-written with Rosemary J. Kind)

A Year Of Ideas:
365 sets of writing prompts and exercises

Short story collections –

Over The Garden Fence
Up The Garden Path
In The Garden Air

No Family Secrets
Can't Choose Your Family
Keep It In The Family
Family Feeling
Happy Families

All That Love Stuff
With Love And Kisses
Lots Of Love
Love Is The Answer

Slightly Spooky Stories I
Slightly Spooky Stories II
Slightly Spooky Stories III
Slightly Spooky Stories IV

Just A Job
Perfect Timing
A Way With Words
Dressed To Impress
Coffee & Cake
Criminal Intent

Printed in Great Britain
by Amazon